This story is based off of unrelated true events

ONE PISSED-OFF SHARK

OFF SHARK

ZACK SCOTT

for my sister
she thought there was a shark in our pool

PROLOGUE

Our tale is not about the origin of the beast.

Our tale is not about the anger in the beast.

Our tale is about seven friends in their late teens and early twenties. Seven very stereotypical friends. Ready to meet them? Good, because neither am I.

First, we have Ray Barren: a levelheaded athlete who is blessed with good looks and a charming personality, traits which helped him win over his lover, Anna Kane, the second person in the group of friends. Given this lovely couple is white, wealthy and attractive, they will most likely survive the shark.

Next, we have Delford "Del" Young. He is Ray's best friend. He is black. He dies first.

William "Willie" Vaughn is a chubby one, a funny fat guy. His blubbery meat in the ocean is like serving a delicious meal on a gold platter to the man-eating beast that is oh so very angry. However, Willie has one trick up his sleeve that just might ensure his survival: he has substantial knowledge regarding sharks.

Then we have Ezekiel "Zeke" Randall. Ah, Zekey Poo, such a hopeless romantic who has been in and out of many relationships, trying to find that special someone. This is why he is hopeless yet romantic. But Zeke has a deep dark secret, which is the reason he fails at love, a secret I will tell you right now:

Zeke is a chronic masturbator.

Sixth, we have Victoria "Vicki" Swatkins. This girl is hot, like smoking hot. She is also quite the sex goddess and will likely get with Zeke or Del or Willie or Anna or Ray or even the seventh friend I haven't mentioned yet or maybe the whole gang at once. Simply put, Vicki only serves one purpose: some good ole T & A.

Last, we have Trisha McCormick—see I told you there are seven friends. She is the opposite of Vicki, a complete prude who doesn't put out for anyone or take off any of her clothes. She doesn't like anything, really, and is basically one of those hipster kids who think they're cool because they're independent thinkers. She is also the youngest of the group. One might think Trisha is a very boring character. Well, whoever "One" is, you're correct. However, like Zeke, she has a dark secret, one no one will expect coming, one that will even stump "One."

If you aren't confused yet, just wait, you will be.

And who am I? My name is Elijah Augustus. Two people in the world call me Eli and you can be the third. I'm a shark hunter. Albeit a self-proclaimed shark hunter, a shark hunter nonetheless.

I hate them beasts and want to rip all their fins off with my teeth.

But I digress. You're probably ready to hear about a shark eating young folk, so there you have it:

Seven friends. Seven friends embarking on a daring journey to go SNUBA diving very close to shore.

Very close to death and danger.

Very close to…

ONE PISSED-OFF SHARK

act one

BROTHERS

The surface was so calm, Billy Billings wanted to lay back, shut his eyes and dream of Miranda Pollock's cute nose.

Calmness died, killed by screams.

"Help!" cried his older brother.

Billy spun his red kayak around with his paddle, slicing into the dark blue ocean. His heart raced as he watched his brother Sebastian's flailing splashes. Sebastian clambered at his yellow kayak but it floated away every time he touched it. Eventually he gave up.

"Hang on, Bass," Billy said so quietly only a nearby seagull could hear him.

By the time Billy reached his brother, Sebastian was underwater. He struck his freckly pale arm around Sebastian's plump shoulder and lifted. There was so much splashing before his brother was heaving for air.

"You okay, Bass? What happened?"

Sebastian wiped his drenched red hair off his face. His gray board shorts were up to his groin, revealing a pink gash in his flesh. "I think a ray got me."

"Stinger or mouth?"

"I think just the mouth." The seventeen-year-old chuckled. "Doesn't really hurt too bad."

"Jesus, Bass, I thought you were actually hurt."

Water splashed off his hair and nailed Billy in the face

as he shook his head. "Well, I can't help I get scared easily. I don't come out here every day like you."

"Yeah, you're always inside playing your magic games."

"Not magic games," wheezed Sebastian. "They are social fantasy games. I'm a level 30 warlock." The chubby teen stopped himself and hung his head. "Damn, I'm a nerd."

"Nerds are cool, yo."

Once again, the surface calmed.

Billy loved being out there—the smell, the sea, the air —he was out there almost every day like Sebastian had said, but after his brother had given him a scare, he wanted to return to shore and drink some cucumber water. He looked at Sebastian. "We aren't going anywhere till you get your kayak. So get off mine, you warlock!"

Billy pushed his brother and was surprised he didn't budge. With their arms locked together, they rocked back and forth, the sea splashing around them.

Knowing the inevitable would happen, Billy cried out, "Stop! You'll make us—"

Both boys flipped into the ocean.

Billy kicked underwater and quickly got a strong hold on his kayak. He paddled around and searched for his brother.

About twenty yards away was Sebastian's yellow kayak. It floated alone.

"Bass!" Billy tried to relax after screaming a couple more times, figuring his brother was playing a prank. He waited for what felt like way too long.

No Bass.

Continuing to tread water, he pressed his face against red plastic and hid from the world, whispering to himself, "This prank needs to end." He then shouted his brother's name, hoping.

"Billy!"

Billy spun to the voice. His brother was on the yellow kayak, waving his fat arms around.

"Miss me?" Sebastian laughed, kicking his legs like he was satisfied with himself. The ocean splashed to his knees as he giggled.

Preparing to compose himself, Billy searched for the calm within the sky, the sea, and the—

His brother screamed again.

Sebastian was flailing, letting out a wail and grabbing at his legs, nearly toppling off his kayak into the ocean.

To Billy's surprise, when his brother yanked his arms out of the ocean, he was holding a large jellyfish. Its pink bell-shaped hood fell on Bass's plump lap and its tentacles and oral arms wrapped around his flesh.

Sebastian cried in pain as he heaved the jellyfish off him.

Billy's eyes locked onto his own paddle floating feet away. He threw his body and swam for it as he pulled his kayak using one hand.

The painful screams of his brother continued to strike his ears.

"Hang on, Bass!"

"First a sting ray," Sebastian yelled. "Now a frackin' jellyfish? I just want to go home!"

Instead of home, Sebastian was sent into the air, spinning until he belly flopped into the ocean.

A lifetime passed as the yellow kayak dropped back to the water. An eerie silence floated in the clouds, floated peacefully, floated quietly. Then came the crashing splash, and with it, Billy's reality.

Rushed onto his knees, he balanced himself on his kayak as he tilted side to side. Although his voice was gone, he yelled his brother's name until a gulp silenced him.

The dark shadow was massive, a pit of black as it

glided beneath him.

Blood followed it.

Had a shark eaten his brother? He tried to fight such craziness from his mind. He'd been out there almost every day and had never once seen a shark.

When blue turned red around him, as if wine had flooded the sea, he knew his nightmare real and he cried for his brother.

Hopeless cries from a hopeless boy.

Powerless against the massive creature, Billy sat frozen on his kayak, staring at the bloody surface. The pale flesh of his brother's leg rose from the depths. Bone stuck out of the severed-off limb.

Billy fell on his butt. What could he do? The shark was at least twenty-five feet long, he guessed. Then a new thought burned his mind. *What if it comes back?*

With strong and determined hands, Billy took his paddle, stabbed the red water and glided to his brother's leg. He held dearly onto what was left of Sebastian. The leg was cold, slippery, and it nearly fell back in the ocean as Billy struck the paddle side to side.

Get home, he told himself. *Get home and save what's left of my bro—*

In a single swift bite, the shark took Sebastian's leg from Billy's lap and then vanished into the dark hole whence it came.

FRIENDS

Ray Barren pulled his silver SUV parallel to a suburban street curb shadowed by large palm trees swaying under the glowing sun.

In front of him was a row of blue and green trash cans. *Blue and green. Blue and green up the entire street.* To Ray's side, a narrow driveway led to a house hidden by a wall of shrubbery.

Ray hated shrubbery. He wanted to throw a fist through all the shrubbery in the world. He also hated trash cans, especially blue and green trash cans. His hands tightened on the steering wheel as he stared at all those damn blue and green trash cans.

From the back seat, Zeke asked, "Shouldn't we call him?"

"No. We have more important things to discuss." Ray's voice seemed sincere, but there was a lightness to it that would likely raise his friend's suspicion.

Zeke scratched the side of his head under his dark blond hair gelled into a fohawk. His skin was paler than Ray's own so it easily turned red from the scratches. "Like what?"

"Like telling me why you and Haley broke up. Anna wants to know." Ray glanced up at the rearview mirror from the driver seat and stared at his own reflection for a second. He had high and tight, dark brown hair. His tan, freckly face helped calm himself down. *I look good today. I look good most days*, he thought.

"Tell me, Zeke. Why the two of you break up?"

"I… not now."

Ray sighed. "Then call Del, you snatch."

"Sorry, man. I didn't bring my phone."

"Why not?"

"'Cause that bitch broke up with me. I didn't need the temptation to call her."

"Seriously, what happened?"

Pink skin darkening, Zeke blinked away from Ray. "It's, uh, complicated."

"I thought you were apathetic to the whole thing?"

"Well shit, man, I didn't want to get dumped, and it's not my fault I like to… never mind." He cleared his throat. "Can we just call Del and get going?"

"Just tell me, Ezekiel!"

"She said she couldn't date a chronic masturbator. That's the reason she left me, fool. You happy?"

Ray tilted his head. "Wait, what?"

In a frustrated frenzy, Zeke waved his hands around as he shifted in his seat and explained, "A chronic masturbator is someone who—"

"I know what chronic masturbating is. What I don't get is why did she break up with you over it? Did you just jerk it and not pay attention to her?" Ray touched Zeke's leg, speaking in a concerned tone. "Was it the porn, Ezekiel? *Was it the porn*? If so, I'm pretty sure they have groups for that."

Zeke swiped his hand away. "Screw you, Rayday. Just call Del."

Laughing hard, Ray had to cough his way to a stop, and his face turned red in the process. He pulled out his cell phone but before dialing, said, "Hey, when Del gets here, do me a favor and don't bring up the whole med school thing, all right? I don't need him getting into one of his moods."

"Don't even know what you're talking about."

One thing Ray liked about Zeke was the guy rarely took anything seriously, unlike Delford who seemed to get butt-hurt about the smallest of things.

A tall, built, and ripped beefcake, Del approached Ray's SUV. He wore dark blue jeans and a red T-shirt. A pair of large sunglasses covered most his face below his dark bald head, making him look like a wannabe diva.

Zeke poked out of the back passenger window. "You dressed for a night of clubbing, Deli-man?"

Irritated already, Del clenched his lips. "There are no rules on how to dress for a boat, Ezekiel."

"You're right. Just, I mean I know black people don't like to swim, but—"

"Screw you, dude!" Del turned his back to Zeke and folded his ripped arms. "No race jokes for once."

"Come on, man. After all our years of friendship, you should know I'm going to crack a couple racial jokes."

Ray shook Del's hand. "He does make a point."

"Yeah, whatever. Where the girls at?"

"Hanging out at that pub by the docks. I always forget its damn name. We're gonna grab them now."

Zeke clapped his hands together. "I guess I'm free to get with Vicki, eh?"

Del turned around in his seat. "You and Haley broke up? What happened?"

"Uh. Can we focus on the inappropriateness of my humor instead?"

Ray let out a wheezing laugh, which almost turned into a choke. "Let's just get to the boat, boys. We have to do this world a favor and party our asses off."

Del raised a fist. "Triple P style."

"Amen," Zeke said.

The boys headed for the docks.

HUNTER

"I want whiskey in one glass, tequila in another," the hunter said.

"That all?" the bartender asked.

"No, sugar nips. Another glass with more whiskey, another with rum."

"So the four glasses. On the rocks? Or?"

The hunter slammed his fist down on the wooden bar. "I want the four glasses, all full, no rocks, no salt, no baby seals. I want nothing in them."

"Two whiskies, a tequila, and rum. Coming right up."

The hunter grew giddy. "Then give me the biggest glass you have."

"For?"

"To mix it all together, *Brian*. You're such a muff-face sometimes."

Bartender Brian turned his back to the hunter, muttering to himself, "I love having you here, asshole."

At the hunter's side, a couple of young girls laughed, but he didn't face them, keeping a forward stare as Brian poured his drinks. Then his upper lip rose as one of the girls approached.

"You really drinking that?" she asked, her voice soft and sweet. "What do you call it?"

"Want a taste?"

He could tell by her scent she was in her midtwenties. Dark brown hair hung past her shoulders, and her bubbly eyes complimented her tan skin. She wore a low cut, black tank top that exposed the cleavage of her average breasts. Squishy. A jean skirt hugged her toned legs. She whispered, "Maybe I do want a taste."

"Come back, Vicki," her friend called out to her.

Ignoring the friend, the hunter looked at the squishy girl. "You couldn't handle this, Vick."

Brian put four glasses down on the bar and slid them to the hunter, then lifted a tall glass from below and put it next to the drinks. He muttered, "Enjoy."

The hunter poured the first glass of whiskey into the tall glass, followed by the tequila, then the rum and finally the second glass of whiskey. Alcohol nearly spilled over the rim.

"I soooo could handle that," stated Vicki in drunk confidence. "What's your name?"

"Why are you over here?"

The girl leaned on him. "I find you interesting, and you look like Mel Gibson from the first *Lethal Weapon*, which is hot. So I'll ask again, what is your name?"

The hunter raised the glass to his lips and chugged, ignoring the squishiness on his arm.

Before Vicki knew it, the drink vanished down the man's throat. He slammed the glass on the wooden bar and turned to her. "You don't want my name."

"Why not?"

"I only want one thing, and you aren't it, princess."

"Oh yeah?" Vicki swung her hair back and angled her breasts at him. "You sure?" She enjoyed toying with older men, though she wasn't sure why. Maybe she was bored, or maybe she thought it funny, either way, it was usually entertaining.

She eyed the man down. He was in his late thirties,

she guessed, wore a bright pink sleeveless shirt and green shorts over his hairy thighs. His skin was a sunburnt tan, and he had a mane of dark brown puffy hair that hung to his shoulders.

"Most guys would buy me a drink by now," she said to him.

The hunter didn't even look at her, which pissed her off.

Pulling away from him, she said, "I'm probably the hottest thing you've talked to in years."

"You know it, young tits."

Vicki cursed and was about to head back to her friend….

Why do they always linger? wondered the hunter. He was not a friendly man, nor an attractive man, nor a hygienic man.

"Vicki!" her friend called out again. "Ray and the others are waiting for us."

"Hang on, Anna." Vicki touched the hunter on his hand, reminding him of that time when he punched a fish in the gills.

"Yes?" he growled, while staring at the bottles of alcohol in front of him.

"You said there's only one thing you want. It's not a hot piece of ass, so what is it?"

The hunter raised a finger to the bartender.

"Same thing?" asked the stupid man.

Frozen and emotionless, the hunter did nothing but stare. As expected, Brian got the hint and prepared the next round. He muttered to himself again, "At least you're a good tipper."

Next to the hunter, Vicki didn't budge. "So?"

"Why do you care?"

"I just want to know. Tell me. What's the one thing you want?"

Anger burned the hunter's voice. "I'm on the hunt for a beast. A beast that lurks this sea. A beast that has no regard for life and devours what it pleases."

Vicki snorted into laughter.

The bartender slid four glasses of alcohol to the hunter again and a tall glass.

Drink made. Chugged. Gone.

Vicki leaned back. "Seriously? Your liver must be messssed up, dude."

The hunter gripped the tall glass so tightly he thought it might shatter within his palm. He'd welcome the blood. He let out a howl and chucked the glass past Vicki's face, almost hitting her friend Anna. It shattered against a tiki post holding up the roof of the bar.

The hunter leaped to his feet and hovered over the girl. "You ever come face-to-face with a shark?" He rubbed his finger down a long scar running from the side of his skull, down his face. The scar was whiter than the rest of his crisped skin.

Vicki backed away, but the hunter struck his paw around her wrist and pulled her into him.

"Stop!" she pleaded.

They always plead when they know the real me. The hunter ignored her cry, for she had to know the truth. "This beast, it hunts this coast and has taken at least two swimmers now. Have you not heard?"

Brian smacked the bar. "Hey!" He slid another tall glass at the man, one already full of various alcohols. "Enough."

The hunter let go of Vicki, looked at the glass, and spat a chunk of saliva into the drink. "I mix my own."

"Take it or leave it, Eli. And behave yourself, you dirty asshole."

Eli growled at the bartender. "You always were a pants-full-of-pussy, Brian."

Both men laughed.

To his side, Vicki rubbed her wrist but didn't move away from him. "Your name is Eli?"

The hunter ignored her.

"Come on, who are you?"

Anna marched over, grabbed her friend and said, "Let's go."

He didn't notice if the girls left because Vicki's questions brought back haunting flashes of sharp white teeth. With little choice now, the hunter knew he'd have to chug down that muckitty-fuckitty mixture of a drink Brian made him.

And so he did, spit and all.

GIRLS

Anna Kane stepped out of the Tiki Pub and Grill. Her long strawberry-blonde hair blew with the ocean breeze as her feet sank in the warm sand. She stared at the calm water in the distance near the docks of the yacht club.

Vicki stumbled out to the beach behind her. "Man, that guy was intense." She fixed the short jean skirt hugging her tan thighs and hiccupped. "Where's Ray Ray?"

"Vick, it's only noon. You drunk?"

"Hey, you took me to a bar."

"Yeah, to eat. Anyway, Ray will be here soon with the boys."

Vicki flashed her straight teeth. "Oh yeah? Ezekiel and Delford, right?"

"I know, you're excited, and Zeke invited his friend William so you should have your hands full."

"Hey!" Vicki let out a little drunk giggle. "I'm not that big of a whore."

"You sure?"

"Bitch!" She laughed and pulled the sleeve of Anna's unzipped white jacket hanging over her pink bikini.

"I, uh," Anna said, "also invited my cousin Trisha."

Her friend's shoulders sank. "What? She's no fun. She always be judging me."

"I know but she wanted to come, and my dad would've been angry if I didn't invite her. She will be fine, though. I promise."

"Whatever you say, Anna Montana. Just get me to the boat so we can start this party."

Trisha Donaldson exited her BMW. Her long black hair swung to her skinny waist, under a large beanie hanging off the back of her head. She pulled out her duffle bag and as she did, scraped her calf on the door. Her curse was silent and of short-lived pain.

"Trish!" Anna yelled, running up from behind.

They were in a cement parking lot overlooking the beach and yacht club.

Trisha spun around, a large smile masking her boney face. "Anna!" They hugged. Her smile vanished when she saw Anna's friend. "Victoria."

"Miss Trisha." Vicki didn't look at her. Typical.

The three girls stood in awkward silence for several seconds.

"Well then." Anna clapped her fingers together. "Let's get our things and get back down to the dock." As she pulled away from the other girls, her phone vibrated in the pocket of her white jacket.

"Hey, babe," she answered. "Ray?" She tilted her head to the side as she looked at the other two girls. "Baby, wait, *hey*, what's wrong?"

Great, Trisha thought. *Ray is having another one of his moments.*

Del and Zeke were in Ray's SUV, watching him pace back and forth outside of it. He didn't care if they watched, was too angry to care as he waved his hands around, yelling into his mobile phone. He eventually hung up and hung his head too.

He dialed again to reach Anna. "No, listen. My dad

said we can't take the yacht. We gotta take the piece-of-shit sailboat."

Anna tried to calm him down on the other end.

"Just listen!" He grabbed his forehead. "Look sorry, babe. I know, I know you hate when I'm like this." He shut his eyes and breathed. "Wait at the yacht club and we will come get you then head to the other docks. Yeah. I'm fine. I love you."

After ending the call, Ray glanced down at his phone. His hand trembled around it. He couldn't help but slam the phone into concrete, shattering it in half.

"Whoa!" both Zeke and Del yelled from inside the SUV.

Ray kicked and stomped pieces of his phone.

Del rushed over to him and grabbed his arm. "Dude, what are you doing?"

Growling, Ray pulled away. "My dad has been on me about everything lately and just, man, I wanted to take the yacht. Not the damn sailboat."

"Come on, Ray, no need to get angry." One of Del's dumb smiles crossed his lips. "It's just a boat."

His head poking out of the SUV, Zeke said, "Be happy, Ray. We're three prongs of a power plug, baby."

"Yeah," he mumbled. "The Triple P."

Waiting at the docks for the boys, Trisha stared at the shallow waters of the ocean. She'd never been a big fan of the sea because the risks of going in it far outweighed the rewards, but Anna had convinced her to join her and her friends. Trisha had never met any of them before except Ray and Vicki.

Vicki. I can't stand her. By the docks on a pebble beach, Anna and Vicki were standing ankle deep in the water. They laughed about something, and Trisha half expected Vicki was making fun of her. Did she care? A little bit. But she didn't want to. She hated caring about other people's opinions. Yet for some reason, Vicki really bothered her, and easily. Perhaps she was just overly protective of her older cousin Anna, and Vicki seemed like one of the worst influences ever.

Unable to pinpoint the exact cause of her anxiety, Trisha hoped the next two days at sea ended quickly.

PREACH

Ray led the group of friends across the rocky wooden dock, under the beaming hot sun. Dozens of various sailboats were spread around them but at the end of the dock was a giant, white wooden sailboat, the name **THE PREACHER** painted across its side in dark blue.

Anna grabbed her boyfriend's arm. "Baby, this boat is beautiful."

"It's not like the yacht," he grumbled.

Del chuckled next to them. "Ray gotta get his way."

A little bit behind Ray, Anna, and Del, Zeke walked with Vicki and Trisha. He hoped Ray wasn't going to be an angry jackass the entire trip.

The guy just needs a cool dip in the ocean, Zeke thought.

"So how you been, Zekey poo?" Vicki asked, fluttering her long dark eyelashes at him.

On his other side, Trisha groaned. He looked down at her. "What?"

She pushed past them, muttering, "Just wear a condom."

"What's her deal?" Zeke asked.

"She's a cunt," Vicki said.

Zeke snorted. "Yikes. Tense."

"Sorry. I hate that word, but, eh, long story."

"We're on a boat for two days if you want to tell it."

Her smile was bright and clean. "Maybe I will."

"Maybe I'll listen."

Vicki winked. "So I heard you and Haley broke—"

Fumbling footsteps ran up behind him, and a familiar voice yelled, "Zeke!"

"Who is that?" Vicki asked.

"Oh, you don't know?" Zeke said in a playful tone. "We have a funny fat friend."

Willie's fluffy brown hair bounced around as he fumbled with duffle bags strapped to his shoulders and a SNUBA raft slung over his back. The bottom of the raft almost hit the wooden dock.

"What's up, Willie man?" Zeke greeted.

Before he said anything, Willie froze in place and stared at Vicki like he'd never seen a girl before. His eyes looked locked to her tan cleavage rising out of a black tank top.

Zeke lowered his head to try and get his friend's attention. "Buddy? Willie?"

Willie's eyes wouldn't leave Vicki, so Zeke yelled at him a couple more times. When Willie jolted to reality, he said to Vicki, "Hi."

"What you got there?" Vicki asked him.

Fumbling with the gear, he said, "Anna likes to SNUBA dive, so I got SNUBA gear from my guy."

"Your guy?"

His smile was fat and dorky. "Yeah. SNUBA isn't available for sale to the public, but I got a guy."

She laughed then left the boys to join the others.

Willie's jaw dropped an inch as he watched her walk away. "Dude, I think I'm in love."

"You're not serious. Right?"

"No, man. I am. Haven't you ever heard of love at first sight?"

"No," said Zeke. "Only lust at first sight."

"Whatever, you cynical poophead." He nodded at The Preacher. "This our boat?"

"Yep."

"There're seven of us, yeah?" Willie was already chuckling when he said, "Don't we need a bigger boat?"

Zeke didn't laugh. "You would."

Although Ray was angry about not taking the yacht, the sailboat wasn't some little dinky thing. It was built in the 1960s and had three decks.

The interior lower deck consisted of multiple berths to sleep on, a small galley and a head. Ray remembered when he was a kid he had pooped in his bathing suit, and tried to rush out of the interior to get on the main deck so he could hop into the water. But when he had climbed onto the tiny ladder, he'd slipped and fallen on his butt.

He laughed at that memory, thinking how pathetic of a kid he'd been.

Sitting on the upper deck of the boat, Ray was behind the captain's wheel in the cockpit. He watched his friends below him on the main deck setting up the SNUBA gear. Anna seemed very excited, which almost made him forget about the yacht. Dressed in a pink bikini, she walked along the edge of the boat, running her hand along rope designed to keep silly people from falling overboard. She passed the front mast and examined its lowered sail. The sail attached to the middle mast also wasn't raised.

At Ray's side, Vicki climbed up a four-foot ladder leading from the main to the upper deck. "So how does this thing work?" Vicki asked as she leaned over him, the top of her breasts near his face.

He couldn't tell if she was coming on to him or just oblivious.

Or, perhaps she simply didn't care.

When she looked at the largest mast, she pointed and said, "Aren't those thingies supposed to go up?"

Ray laughed. "Those *thingies* don't have to be raised. We're being propelled by an engine." He slapped the throttle.

Vicki raised her head and widened her eyes. "Gotcha. I know nothing about boats or scuba diving."

"Luckily for you"—he pointed at himself—"the captain does know something about boats. And we aren't scuba diving. It's SNUBA."

"SNUBA? That's like scuba diving and—"

"Snorkeling."

He'd never been a big fan of Vicki because she was always getting into trouble and he feared her actions would somehow influence his Anna. But luckily, and sometimes he had to remind himself, Anna was a strong girl.

"Anna loves to SNUBA," he said. "You should help her set up. She'll teach you a few things, and we're almost to our spot."

Vicki looked away from Ray. He'd always been good to Anna, but for some reason, she found the guy too full of himself to be likable.

"Yeah, I don't think I'm the SNUBA diving type," she said to him.

In the short distance, she still clearly saw the shore. People were enjoying the beach, kids ran around, dudes hit on babes, and as much as she wanted to be with her friends, she would've rather felt the sand between her toes and a warm towel against her back.

"Land isn't far away," she said. "We can't be that close to our diving spot, right?"

"We aren't going too far out. Like I said, no scuba for us."

She wiped strands of hair off her face. "So do you love SNUBA, too?"

Leaning back in the captain's chair, Ray touched her

wrist. "I love Anna."

"How sweet."

"We will find that perfect guy for you someday, Vicki."

Yeah. Sure. Vicki wasn't a fan of the whole 'love' thing because she thought it made people do stupid things, but she kept that opinion to herself and said, "Let's just have a good time."

The cabin of the sailboat was dark, musky, and had mahogany furnishings. Willie thought it was classy as fuck. He stepped into the galley and touched the stove, then played with the sink faucet, then put one foot on a cooler like he'd just conquered the place.

After getting a good feel for his surroundings, Willie opened the cooler's white lid and brought out three bottles of beer, then joined Zeke and Trisha at a small table situated between two berths tucked into the sides of the cabin. It was quite cozy. He handed the first beer to Zeke then leaned the other toward Trisha.

"I don't drink," she said.

"Whoa." Zeke raised his hands at her. "Watch out, we got a saint hurr."

"I'm just careful about what I put in my body, and when I put it in."

"Hot."

When she turned her focus to Willie, he thought she believed him more civil than Zeke. "What's Anna doing?" she asked.

Zeke answered for him, "She's setting up the SNUBA stuff."

"Isn't it your job, William?"

"Hey, I just brought the stuff. I don't really know how to use it."

Trisha moved for the ladder leading up to the main deck. The sunlight glowing behind her made her a silhouette as she said, "Well, good thing we have my cousin then." She climbed out of the cabin.

"Damn, dude." Zeke slid next to Willie. "She's uptight."

Willie's cheeks jiggled as he tilted his beer at Zeke. "To the tight ones."

Their glasses clanked.

The large inflatable SNUBA raft had a white bottom, light blue stripes around the top, safety lanyards along the sides, and hoses with regulators at the end of them to breathe through.

It's cool looking, Ray thought as he stood on the upper deck, *but just give me a mask and some fish to watch. None of this fancy crap.*

Crouched over the raft, Anna pushed a large black bag toward Del and told him to pull out the gear. The bag was full of masks, snorkels, and fins.

"We got wetsuits?" Del asked.

Anna shook her head. Her strawberry-blonde hair was pulled back in a ponytail. "Suck it up, Del, it's not that cold."

He laughed. "You're a tough one. Never knew you were into this."

Anna waved a hand playfully.

"Seriously, girl, if we got stranded out here, and only one of us survived, it'd for sure be you."

"Knock it off."

Ray smiled at Del's statement and thought the same thing. Anna was a badass who took shit from no one, though most people would never think it because she was so kind and looked like the innocent girl next door.

"Okay," Del said. "So how does this diving stuff work?"

"The SNUBA raft gives us air through these lines." Anna lifted a bright yellow hose. "Then we breathe through the regulator. No need for any tanks on our backs."

"Sweet. How far down can we go?"

"About twenty feet." Anna peeked into the bag as Del opened it. "Willie didn't pack weight belts? Damn. So maybe not twenty feet. Depends on your swimming skills."

Just then, Trisha climbed out of the interior of the sailboat. "Is it safe? The SNUBA?"

"Perfectly safe," Ray stated as he hopped down from the upper deck. He helped Vicki by holding her waist and lowering her to the wooden floor. "Nothing to fear in there but man-eating turtles."

Trisha's eyebrows furrowed. "Man-eating turtles?"

Remembering how literal Trisha could be, Ray ignored her and smiled at Del. "Help me with the anchor?"

The two of them went to the front of the boat, which floated steadily on the calm surface.

"How you doing, Del?" Ray asked.

"Good, man, why?"

"The whole med school thing. If you want to talk about it, I'm here for you."

"How bout we just have fun these next two days, yeah?"

After leaving medical school, Del had become a different guy. He was not as confident as he used to be and it seemed like his manhood had been severely damaged because any little comment had a good chance of hurting his feelings.

Ray hoped the trip would bring his friend back to his normal, confident self. Preparing to release the anchor, he said, "You got it, buddy. Just fun."

SNUBA

Ray, Anna, Del, Willie, Zeke, Vicki and Trisha stood on the main deck of the sailboat around the SNUBA gear. Del still wore his dark blue jeans and red shirt, so Trisha asked him, "Are you swimming in that?"

"His kind doesn't know how to swim," Zeke said under his breath,

Del struck a finger at Zeke. "Hey, screw you, man. I brought some board shorts. Let me change and show you how good I am. I bet I swim better than you."

"Yeah, I'm not going in there."

Ray raised a bushy brown eyebrow. "Why not?"

"In case you guys didn't know, two people have been killed by a great white shark in the last month or so around here," Zeke explained. "I fucking hate sharks."

Willie raised a hand. "Those were freak occurrences. Sharks don't like the taste of us. Plus, Delford here is black, so he'd get eaten first, leaving the rest of us to survive."

Del stomped on the deck. "Enough with the black jokes!" He then glanced at Willie's shirtless chubby chest and belly. "You shouldn't make fun of people, Will, you have pepperoni nipples."

Everyone glanced down at Willie's large red nipples and cracked into laughter. His face grew bright red, almost as red as his nips. He tried to play off a fake laugh, but his voice tightened. "I have a deficiency!"

During the laugh fest, Vicki glanced up at Zeke. "If you're staying, so am I."

Trisha didn't want to let them screw around up there by themselves. Maybe that was selfish of her, or she was a little jealous, but Vicki had to learn to keep her pants on. She didn't mind giving her the assist. "Yeah, I think I'll stay, too."

"Why?" Anna asked. "You said you would try this."

"Someone has to look after the kids."

Anna, wearing a bright pink bikini, leaped into the cool water. She waved at Ray to lower the SNUBA raft from the sailboat. He did so, then dove in.

They were the first two in the ocean, and swam around one another, smiling and splashing.

Anna was about to grab Ray like she wanted to kiss him, when Willie yelled, "Cannonball!" He hopped off the boat and the splash caused the SNUBA raft to dart away from the group.

Ray groaned, swam from Anna, and grabbed the raft. When he turned around, he was a lot farther from the group than he expected. "I got it!"

By himself paddling in place, he glanced around the calm surface and wished he could be as calm, but his chest burned with an urge to smack Willie across the face.

Over a stupid cannonball? Ray knew he needed to learn how to relax, to not let little things heat him up. So he pulled his mask over his face and swam back to the group.

Anna handed him a regulator. "You ready, babe?"

"Absolutely."

Willie splashed his way to the SNUBA raft, and the three swimmers looked up at Del, who was standing at the edge of the sailboat by the rope ladder leading down to the water.

Del stared at his friends, his legs shaking. He had no idea why he was so nervous. He even wondered where his balls were. *I'm not a coward. I'm not.*

Before sticking the regulator in her mouth, Anna yelled to him, "Jump in!"

Del raised a hand. He was shirtless and in yellow board shorts. "One second. Gotta fix my trunks and—"

Rushing footsteps cut him off. He flew forward, shrieking and flailing in the air until crashing into the sea. Resurfaced, he threw a fist at the boat. "EZEKIEL!"

Zeke didn't know why he liked messing with Del so much. He loved the guy, sure, but teasing him was very enjoyable. Slapping his legs and laughing, Zeke said, "I'm sorry, buddy. The temptation consumed me."

"Just wait till I get back up there, you dick."

He raised his hands by his face and shook them. "Ooo, so scared."

As he mocked his friend, a footstep caused him to spin. Vicki shoved her hands at him, but he pushed forward, colliding into her, shoving her down onto the wooden deck.

Two bodies entangled, Zeke's chest heaved above her.

"Oh, kinky." Vicki smiled.

He smirked and was about to lean in for a kiss.

Trisha cleared her throat.

Pushing off her and rolling onto his back, Zeke stared up at Trisha. "Sorry, Mom."

"You an asshole to all your friends?"

He touched his chest, right above his heart. "Only to the ones I love."

Trisha groaned and turned around. Her beanie

nearly fell off the back of her head, but she caught it.

Vicki was still lying on the main deck next to Zeke, and she said to him, "Man, I hate hipsters."

Her smile was so bright, he wanted to feel her lips on his.

Willie, Ray, Anna, and Del floated around the SNUBA raft.

"A couple of things before we go under," Anna started after pulling the regulator from her mouth. She lifted a hand vertically over her head. "Do this if you see a shark." She then sliced her hand across her neck. "This if you must go back to the boat. Got it?"

"Anything else, my beautiful guide?" Ray asked.

"Just have fun, dolls." Anna dove under first, followed by Ray then Del.

Willie waded in place for a few more moments, watching Zeke and Vicki talking to each other up on the boat. They waved at him, and he did the same, hoping Zeke would put a good word in for him.

I would do anything to be with that girl, he thought. *But first I need to go look at some fishies.*

When he peeked in the water, he spotted various fish swimming near Ray and Del. He whispered to himself, "Beneath this glassy surface, a world of gliding assholes."

With the regulator in his mouth, he descended.

UNDER

Vicki shoved Zeke onto the berth and untied the back of her black bikini top. Her breasts hung freely in front of his face. Straddling him, she pressed her topless body against his chest and whispered into his ear, "Time to forget about your ex." She kissed down his neck, his pecs, his stomach. Using her teeth, she undid the strings of his board shorts.

Zeke fought to keep his eyes open. "I can't believe this is happening."

Vicki laughed and stuck her tongue out at his crotch. "Too bad you're in a dream."

Suddenly, Zeke felt locked. "What?"

A presence hovered near him. Willie, shirtless, rubbed his large pepperoni nipples and said, "You're in a bad dream, my man." He smiled then leaped for Zeke.

Waking up in a pouring sweat, Zeke bumped his head on the V-berth at the back of the cabin. He grabbed his temple and growled, rolling on the cushion. "Shit!"

Trisha was rummaging through the small galley across from him. "You okay?"

"Nightmare, I think."

After finding a little baggie of carrots, Trisha glanced at the tent pitched in his light blue board shorts. "Seemed real scary."

Zeke quickly lowered his hands over his lap. "Uh, so,

how long was I out for? And how the hell did I pass out already?" As he said that, he stared at Trisha in her tankini. She didn't look half bad to him, and he contemplated making a move on her but quickly knew better, thinking she'd likely gut him in his sleep if he acted improperly.

"Not very long," she said. "Vicki is upstairs sunbathing, and the others are still in the water." She pointed at the beer bottle by Zeke's feet. "As for passing out, learn to handle your liquor."

He scratched his neck, thinking he wasn't that much of a lightweight. He was just tired from all the drama with his ex, and the moment he slowed down, he was out. Time seemed to be slipping every second he sat there on the berth, so he shook his head and snapped his attention back to Trisha. "You enjoying yourself or what?"

"Trying to. You seem to be having a blast by yourself."

"I don't know what happened. Guess it's been a long few days."

"Want to talk about it?"

His legs wobbly, Zeke stumbled his way to the table Trisha sat at. "No offense, but not with you."

She crunched a carrot for a few seconds like she was trying to annoy him then swallowed. "No offense taken. Just don't throw me in the water like you did to Del."

"Wouldn't dream of it."

Light broke through the surface, illuminating the blue sea for the four friends.

Ray led Anna, Willie, and Del above a large reef. A few sheepshead fish swam around them; their gray bodies lined with black stripes shimmered in the water. An occasional orange garibaldi would glide underneath them. Ray looked down to his right where a school of sardines sped into his sight then retracted into the shadowy waters in the distance.

He smiled, loving the peace the sea brought him, and he hoped it brought the same peace to Del.

At the rear of the group, Del was excited and worried as he'd never been under the surface of the ocean like that before.

For some reason he kept staring at the dark reaches of the sea, picturing a large shark. His imagination really freaked him out, and he paused in his glide, floating in one spot. His heart racing, he was about to panic, but he shut his eyes and breathed through his regulator. He told himself to be the confident Del he once was.

Upon opening his eyes, he saw the SNUBA raft floating away from him, tugged by his three friends as they swam. Before his tube was pulled from his mouth, he got himself together and followed the others.

Something was behind him. He spun around, his legs kicking, his arms outstretched at his sides. Nothing. Only the dark sea stared at him.

Floating in one spot, air rushing in and out of his body, he stared at the empty beyond of the ocean again. The only thing he heard was the sound of his breath.

Be the confident Del, he told himself. *Be him.*

As he prepared to catch up to his friends, he realized not as many fish were in the area, which didn't help him relax. Still, he fought off the terrifying thoughts trying to consume him.

Then he saw it.

The regulator loosened in his mouth. He panicked for the surface, his hand knocked his mask, and water burned his eyes. His chest felt like something was trying to flatten it but he still managed to grab the SNUBA raft.

Treading in place, Del caught his breath and tried to

get his heart to slow down. Then he remembered that just because he was touching the raft, it didn't mean he was safe.

A nearby splash almost made him cry.

Ray pulled out his regulator and said, "What happened, man?"

Wide-eyed, Del stared at him, his mouth hanging open.

"Delford, what the hell happened?"

Shaking lips couldn't say the word, then Ray slapped him across the face, and Del snapped back to reality.

"*Shark*," he whispered.

SWIM

Anna, Ray, Del, and Willie swam as fast as they could for The Preacher. Anna continued to look below the surface, watching out for the shark. She didn't catch anything except for some familiar fish species they'd seen before.

Even after all the times she'd been in the ocean, diving or snorkeling or swimming, she'd never seen a shark. A part of her wanted to see it, while another part of her wanted to get the hell out of the water.

They were thirty feet from the sailboat.

Ray led the group, swimming with good form while pulling the SNUBA raft with him. Willie was a slower swimmer than Anna, but she stayed behind him to make sure he didn't get separated from the group. Meanwhile, Del made the most splashes as he swam but he was almost as quick as Ray.

Her boyfriend reached the sailboat first. Ray grabbed the rope ladder with one hand, while still holding the raft, and before he climbed he turned back and looked at Anna.

Del splashed up to him, thrashing to get on the boat. His large muscles flexed as he pulled his body out of the water but his fin got caught on the ladder, causing him to slip and slam into the SNUBA raft. Ray couldn't hold onto it.

Anna, farthest from the boat, stared at the escaping SNUBA raft. She paddled away from the group for it and heard Ray yell, "Just leave it!"

She kept swimming, even when someone told her to turn around. Another person yelled at her to look out. When she reached the raft, she looked back to see a dorsal fin breaking the surface behind her.

Ray's throat must've ripped open as he cupped his mouth and screamed, "*ANNA.*"

Knowing she couldn't outswim the creature yards from her, Anna took a deep breath, tried not to panic, and lowered underwater.

The bottle nose of the dolphin greeted her. Gracefully, it circled around her and its gray body must've been about six feet long. Then it swam away as if all it wanted was to say a quick hello.

When Anna came up for air, Ray reached her and said, "You hurt? Where is it?" There was worry in his eyes that she had never seen before.

She wrapped an arm around his shoulders and pressed her cheek against his, and although she was calm, relief filled her words as she whispered, "It was only a dolphin."

Back aboard the boat, Ray shoved Del into one of the masts on the main deck.

Del hoped his friend punched him in the face so he could feel something other than fear, but Willie and Anna rushed between the two of them.

"You're an idiot," Ray said to him. "You ruined all of this over a damn dolphin."

"Man, that was no dolphin I saw."

"How do you even know? You know shit!"

Anna grabbed her boyfriend. "Baby, calm down."

Yanking away from her and turning his back to all of them, Ray tightened his hands into fists. He looked like one wrong word would set him off.

"I'm telling you it was a shark," Del said.

Willie stepped next to him. "What kind of shark?"

Del shrugged.

"Figures," muttered Ray.

"Wait, what did you see exactly?" Willie asked.

Del slightly paced to the side. "The back of it, the uh…."

"Caudal fin," finished Willie.

"Yeah sure. That's what I saw."

"It's quite easy to tell the difference between the back of a shark and the back of a dolphin." Willie looked at everyone else. "Maybe you did see a shark. How big was it?"

"I have no idea. I-I don't know."

Ray laughed. "He probably saw some big harmless fish and freaked out like the pussy he is. Guy can't even stick through med school."

Anna grabbed her boyfriend. "Ray!"

"Okay." Del threw his hands out. "I'm done. I know what I saw. You can all screw yourselves." He rushed into the cabin, slipping on the ladder then hitting the floor.

He stayed sprawled out, listening to the others outside. Some were questioning him, while others came to his defense thinking maybe he had in fact seen a shark. He didn't care because he knew he'd seen it. He knew he'd seen a shark.

However, sharks were the least of his problems. He was falling apart ever since he dropped out of med school, and it was only a matter of time until he crumbled to nothing.

Leaning over the side of the boat, Ray lowered his head and rubbed the back of his neck. He'd wanted so badly to punch Del in the face because of how dumb the guy was being, but he'd controlled himself in front of Anna.

Anna came to him. She was a good girl like that, always looking after him. She said, "You happy now?"

"I'll apologize later. I thought I was going to lose you."

She was so pretty standing there in her little pink bikini, Ray just wanted to hold her, but she beat him to it. Wrapping her arms around his slender waist, she pressed her head against him. He kissed her head, fighting a tear ready to fall from his eye. Together, the two of them stared at the calm waters.

A dolphin leaped from the depths, spiraling in the air, and it was followed by another. They danced under the setting sun.

"Amazing," Anna said.

Ray couldn't care less about the dolphins. For when he held his girlfriend, the anger in his chest extinguished.

On the upper deck, Trisha kept an eye on her cousin Anna, who looked at peace as she enjoyed the dancing dolphins. Trisha wished she could have peace of mind, too, but she believed Del when he'd said he saw a shark. Considering the gang would likely go in the water again, she wondered if maybe they should all just head home that night and not take the chance of swimming into the dangerous creature.

Maybe I'm overthinking this, she wondered.

Next to Ray and Anna, Willie stood by Vicki as they also watched the dolphins. Vicki had a large bright smile that almost made her seem nice. "Beautiful," she said to Willie.

"Yes you are."

Vicki laughed and nudged him. "Think so?"

"Oh yes," he said so quickly he almost sounded like he'd fallen in love right then. "Yes definitely."

Vicki laughed again and rubbed his arm. "Just watch the dolphins."

"I'll watch anything while next to you."

Great, Trisha thought. *He seems nice, Vicki, don't go hurting him.*

Behind the four friends, Zeke stood alone on the main deck with a look on his face like he hated being there, which made Trisha wonder, *Perhaps there's more to him than just being a horny prick.*

Zeke stared at Vicki's ass. He wanted to pull her bikini down, bend her over, and have his way. A tingling beneath his skin urged him to march right over there and take her.

When he glanced down at his shorts, he noticed a slight bulge beneath its strings.

Holy shit, he thought to himself. *What the hell is wrong with me? Why can't I just enjoy my time with friends? Why does it always have to be about butts and boobs?*

Zeke hated those thoughts, so he headed toward the galley in order to distract his mind. For the dolphins could dance, and the sun could set, and his friends could see the beauty in it all, but Zeke just wanted a beer.

PARTY

The air was warm, and everyone was still in their bathing suits, and Anna couldn't imagine a better night with her friends.

A hip-hop song blasted from the boom box situated by some lanterns that dimly lit the main deck. Ray and Anna rubbed against each other to the music, lifting their drinks in the air. Although she didn't need him to be safe, Anna loved how secure she felt with her boyfriend behind her and his hand on her hip.

Next to them were Del and Vicki. Vicki rocked her hips to the slow beat, while he swayed back and forth a few inches from her. His eyes looked like they were penetrating through the light pink cloth tied around her waist, covering her black bikini bottom.

"I'll be right back," Ray whispered into Anna's ear, and before she could say anything, he shouted, "Del. Let's talk."

Del looked away from Vicki and nodded.

With the boys gone, Vicki did some dorky dance move over to Anna and nearly spilled her drink as she slurred, "Let's dance!"

Anna loved Vicki, but the girl was getting a little out of hand with her partying. She guessed she couldn't blame her, though, because Vicki didn't have much going on in her life except for her looks.

She could be so much more, Anna thought, but it would be a thought she'd keep to herself.

The girls danced.

At the bow of the sailboat, Ray looked over the edge at the dark waters. He needed to apologize to Del, but he really was tired of the guy being oversensitive. "Listen," he said, "about what I said earlier, you know, the whole med school thing."

Del raised a hand. "It's fine, bro. Still best friends?"

"Always." Ray looked around the boat. "Where's Zeke? I feel like the three of us need to cheers."

"Yeah. The Triple P."

Ray, Del, and Zeke had known each other since they were kids and went to the same high school and college together. Del had graduated early and went to med school, while Zeke and Ray had moved back home.

On the upper deck of the boat, Zeke raised his beer at the guys. He also held the ship's only flare gun and shouted, "You guys want some fireworks?"

Before Ray could say anything, Zeke fumbled with the gun until it fell off his hands. It vanished into the water. Zeke hung his head and said, "Ray. A mistake was made."

Ray laughed to himself. *Classic Zeke.*

"Shouldn't we try to find it?" Del asked.

"That flare gun was so old it probably didn't work." Straightening his back, Ray smiled and raised his glass. "Let's forget about flares. To you, me, and Zeke."

"Three prongs of a power plug, baby," Del said.

"Triple P." Ray sipped his beer in silent thought for a moment. "But, you know, if you want to talk about school, though, I'm here, bud."

Del drank as he looked at his sandals. "Just couldn't handle it."

"It's okay. I was surprised you went in the first place."

After stating that, Ray instantly regretted his words. "I mean…."

"Yes, Ray, what do you mean?"

"Look, I love you, man, but you're always running from stuff. So I was surprised you'd make such a commitment to something like med school."

Standing at almost the same height, Del squinted at Ray for a disappointing second. "Thanks." He returned to the dancing girls.

"Damn." Ray chugged the rest of his beer. "Sensitive prick."

After raising his beer to his buds, Zeke drank, thinking how much he loved those two fools. And Willie. He loved Willie, who was standing next to him on the upper deck of the boat.

They were watching Vicki dance around in her little black bikini.

"Yep, I'm in love with her," Willie stated.

"You don't even know her. Not to mention she is a big ole whore."

"Oh, whatever. You'd hit that, and you know it, Mr. Chronic Masturbation Man."

"What? Haley told you?"

Willie shrugged. "Look, I was trying to get with her friend Maggie and it slipped out one night."

"That's what she said."

Ignoring the comment, Willie slapped his friend's back. "Don't worry, brother-man, I yank it a lot too. But I wouldn't if I was tapping a girl like Vicki."

Zeke raised a hand. "Willie, you always do this."

"Do what?"

"Act like you're in love with some slutty hot girl. Then when you see them with someone else, you get all heartbroken."

Willie downed some more beer and let out a long airy

burp. "Yes, but I am feeling good about this one. I made her laugh while watching the dolphins."

Zeke groaned. "Whatever. Heads up, though, 'cause I think she's into me."

"Well, you said she's a big ole whore." He put his fingers in quotation marks. "Maybe she will tap us both."

Just then, the two friends heard loud breathing at their side.

"What are you boys talking about?" Trisha asked.

"Oh great," groaned Zeke. "Boner kill."

Willie chuckled.

They sat on cushioned benches behind the cockpit, Trisha next to Zeke, Willie across from them.

"You guys having fun?" she asked.

"Until now, yeah." Zeke smirked at Willie and raised his hand. "Up top."

Trisha punched his arm. He slumped and frowned.

"So what's up, Trish?" wondered Willie.

"I have a question about the whole shark thing."

"It was a dolphin," stated Zeke.

"I'm talking to William. Thank you."

A large smile crossed Willie's face. "Yeah, she's talking to me, sir. Thank you."

"That's my cue." Zeke rose, finished his beer, chucked it overboard then climbed down to the main deck.

Willie crossed his pudgy legs and leaned forward. "Continue, Miss Trish."

Trisha rolled her eyes. "You think Del saw a shark? I mean, you made it sound like it's hard to mistake the back of a dolphin for the back of a shark."

"Yeah, would be pretty hard, but I wouldn't worry about anything."

"Why is that? We are SNUBA diving again tomorrow

and if it's out there—"

"Trish, is it cool if I call you *Trish*? Anyway, if there was a shark, which there could have been, it wouldn't stick around our boat until morning anyway."

"How do you know?"

"Trish, my sweet Trish." He waved his beer around with an idiotic smile. "You have seen one too many shark movies."

Zeke poked his head up from the main deck, standing on his toes. "Shut up, Willie, you love shark movies."

Willie groaned. "Shark movie. Only one. There is only one shark movie I love."

Trisha laughed. "Which?"

"*Deep Blue Sea* of course."

She pressed her hand against her face. "You, William, have lost all credibility. The only shark movie to praise is *Jaws*."

"Thank you!" Zeke called out, then lowered himself from their view.

From somewhere unseen, Ray yelled, "What about *Spring Break Shark Attack*?"

Ignored.

"The *Jaws* sequels suck," Willie argued, "so the original loses credibility."

"But the original is a classic," Trisha said.

Willie shook his head. "Nope! Won't hear it! Now moving on… tell me about your concerns again."

"Well, say Delford saw a shark and say this shark likes hanging around this area. Then it could be dangerous to go back in the water, right? Aren't they territorial? That's all I'm thinking."

Willie looked down at his beer then at Trisha's empty hands. "Are you even drinking tonight? Because if you aren't drunk, I think you might be crazy."

"Ass!" She shot to her feet and turned away from him, but before she could leave, he grabbed her wrist.

"Look, sorry. Talk to me."

"Just, what do you think? I mean, hypothetically, is the shark still here?"

"Well hypothetically," Willie said, "pretend we're in a shark movie. Doesn't matter which one. In that scenario, the shark would likely still be down there, waiting for us."

Trisha nodded.

"In almost all shark movies, hell, in almost any horror movie, there is a prescare before the actual horror happens."

"A prescare?"

"Yes, one that doesn't really harm anyone but leads them to their fates. One might consider it a warning of things to come. A foreshadowing, perhaps." He scratched the side of his head. "The dolphins earlier today…."

Trisha shivered. "That was our prescare. I need another drink." She hiccupped as she walked away.

Willie's eyes widened. "Wait for me!"

Hours later, Anna and Ray collapsed onto the V-berth at the back of the cabin. Ray got on top of her and caressed her face. Their lips touched, and since he'd forgotten his toothbrush, he hoped his breath didn't scare her off.

"You smell like vodka and beer," she said.

"Some say it's an aphrodisiac." He moved his hand right above her elbow, and since he wasn't in the mood for much foreplay, he went straight to the pink top covering her large pale breasts.

When his hand slipped under, Anna stopped him.

"What is it?" Ray whispered, wanting to get the top off so he could feel her bare against him.

"Del and Trisha are sleeping like three feet away."

They could hear Del snoring, so Ray said, "He's out

cold."

"Yeah, but my baby cousin is here."

While her excuse for not wanting to be intimate was reasonable, he thought maybe she was mad at him for something. His anger had gotten in the way of their intimacy before, so maybe his reaction to Del earlier was what did it.

No matter the reason, Ray loved Anna and wanted to share his love with her, so he went for her boob again but she turned onto her side.

"Sorry, baby," she whispered. "Not while my cousin is here."

"Trisha is what? Eighteen? Come on, babe."

"No. Let it go."

"All right. Okay." Although Ray had a terrible time controlling his anger, he did know when to control his desires. So he fell onto his back and said, "If only we took the yacht."

HANGOVER

Throbbing like a motherfucker, Ray's head felt ready to explode. He didn't realize how much he'd drunk last night until he woke up, but he knew getting back in the ocean would help heal him.

It always had.

At his side, the blanket had slid down Anna's legs, revealing her scrunched up bikini. Ray gave her pink butt a light smack, startling her awake.

He smiled down at her. "Time for round two."

"Do we really have to go in the water again? Let's go home," she whispered.

"*We* don't have to do anything, but I'm going out again."

"Why?"

"Why does it matter? Our SNUBA time was cut short 'cause of that idiot." He raised his chin at the snoring Del. "Why don't you want to go in? You love SNUBA."

"I don't know. I just have a bad feeling." She rubbed her temples. "What if Del did see a shark?"

"You're just hungover." He kissed her head. "Dancing dolphins, Anna."

She smiled lightly. "Okay fine, yeah, but if we just go home, we can have our privacy." She reached her hand up his long bare chest. "Sorry we couldn't last night."

Not wanting to get into an argument with her, he

kissed her hand. "Time to get ready."

"Okay, babe."

In the galley, Ray clapped his hands. "Rise and shine, everyone!"

Del groaned awake. "Shit, man, time to wake for what?"

"Hey, don't give me that. The last SNUBA dive of the trip starts in thirty minutes."

"Ray, don't you ever get a hangover?" Del threw a pillow over his bald head. "You drank more than me."

Although he was feeling like shit, Ray would never admit it and said, "I'll get a hangover when I'm dead."

Right when he got onto the main deck, disappointment covered his face. Thick fog surrounded him. Visibility was nearly gone, the land cut off from sight.

Directly to his side lay the passed-out Willie, curled up into a ball in front of the ladder leading to the upper deck. Ray was excited to mess with him, so he stomped the wooden floor and yelled, "Iceberg!"

Willie sprung awake. "No, Ryan Seacrest!"

"What?"

"Huh?"

After standing awkwardly for a second, Ray said, "Never mind. You gonna SNUBA with me? The others are backing out."

"Oh, yeah, sure." He looked around for a few seconds, unfolded his pudgy arms, and a black circular object fell from his grasp.

"My compass!" Ray knelt. The compass was cracked. Useless. "You broke it, you imbecile!"

"Dude, I think I'm still drunk," Willie said.

On the upper deck, Zeke stood like someone had just shocked him awake. He wasn't wearing his shirt and his shorts were undone.

Willie laughed and said, "Have a nice night by

yourself?"

Covered by a blanket, Vicki stumbled up next to Zeke. She yawned and asked what everyone was doing.

"SNUBA time," Ray said.

"Oh forget that." Vicki lowered again, and Zeke followed her.

Hanging his head, Willie sat on the floor like the saddest boy who had ever lived. "Ass," he whispered.

Ray tightened his fin around his ankle, spat into his mask, and rubbed the saliva around, hoping to not get involved with whatever was going on between Willie, Vicki, and Zeke. However, Willie seemed so sad, Ray figured he should comfort a buddy and said, "Dude. What's up?"

"I can't decide if I have the worst hangover ever or if I'm suffering from a broken heart."

Ray cocked his head back. "What are you talking about?"

"Thought I had a chance with Vicki," huffed Willie. "Zeke has her."

Ray snorted. "Trust me, man, you ain't missing much."

Just then, Anna emerged from the interior of the sailboat. She shivered. "Where did this crap weather come from?"

Both boys shrugged.

"You aren't going to see much in this."

Ray fixed the mask over his head. "We will make do." He went to the edge of the boat and sat, hoping Anna would follow him.

She did.

Their legs hung over the edge, and their toes dangled right above the water. The water was a little choppy so the boat rocked up and down, and for some reason it gave Ray a feeling like he shouldn't go in the ocean.

Or maybe he just needed to throw up from the

alcohol.

He placed a hand on Anna's thigh and said, "I'll see you in a bit, babe."

She kissed his cheek. "Come on, let's go home and relax. We can do whatever you want before dinner with my dad. I'll give you a special treat."

Ray enjoyed how stubborn she was to keep him on the boat, especially because it was fun to mess with her. *I'll just go in for a little*, he thought. *Then I'll come give you the longest kiss you've ever felt, darling.*

Ray winked at Anna, then dropped into the ocean.

Trisha's throat was so dry when she woke up; she thought she was choking. Leaning out of the berth, she grabbed a water bottle, drank, and almost instantly felt better.

Across from her, Del snored beneath a pillow. She hoped he was having sweet dreams free of sharks.

After putting on a jacket, Trisha climbed out of the cabin and stood over the sulking Willie. He was struggling to get his fins on. She said, "Uh, William, what about what you said last night?"

He squinted up at her like he was seeing life for the first time. "Huh?"

"You said yesterday was the prescare. That today would be worse."

Willie scratched his fluffy hair and laughed. "Oh, that? I was just messing around. That's all bullshit. This isn't a movie."

"You sure?"

"Yeah, come on, Trish. Did you think I was serious?"

She felt slightly embarrassed because people had always told her she took things too seriously. So she shrugged off the question, and glanced at the gray sky above dark water. "I guess I could join you then."

Willie smiled at her and handed her a snorkel mask.

Then Zeke stumbled onto the main deck.

"What's up, asshole?" Willie greeted. He seemed so sweet, so Trisha was surprised by his tone.

Cringing, Zeke said, "Ah, Willie-man. I didn't mean for this to piss you off. You barely even know her."

Trisha pulled the snorkel mask past her face, so it hung around her neck. She said to Willie, "You wanted Vicki?" She then looked at Zeke. "And you slept with her? *You are an asshole.*"

Willie smiled and thanked her.

After ending her stare-down with Zeke, Trisha moved to the edge of the boat. Ray was in the water, while Anna watched him.

"Why do you hang out with Zeke?" Trisha asked her cousin, making sure that asshole heard her. "He's nothing but a prick."

"Screw you," Zeke said. "You don't know me, you uptight hooker."

"I know you're a chronic masturbating asshole."

"Relax, Trish," Anna said.

Zeke's face burned red as he looked down at Willie. "*You told her?*"

"There wasn't much to tell," Trisha snarled and marched toward Zeke. "You're just a little man with a little penis."

"Shut up, bitch!" He shoved her.

Stronger than he looked, Zeke's push surprised Trisha. But she wasn't that close to the edge of the boat so she knew she'd be okay.

The ocean told her otherwise.

Half his body in the water as he held onto the ladder, Ray watched Trisha flail into the ocean. He'd been waiting for the SNUBA raft when the incident happened.

Trisha resurfaced immediately, screamed and

splashed around. "You dick!" Her beanie was somehow still stuck to her hair. "You asshole, Zeke!"

Ray could hear Zeke giggling up on the boat, and he too laughed.

One stroke over to Ray and Trisha said, "Don't laugh at me. Help!"

Above him, Anna stood at the edge of the boat, smiling. "Well, Ray, help her."

Trisha kept screaming.

"Alright, *all right*," Ray said. "Everyone relax."

Trisha was right next to him. "Just pull me out of the water."

"Okay."

Before he had a chance to grab her, she was gone, leaving only bubbles.

"Trisha?"

Above Ray, Anna asked, "Where did she go?"

White bubbles turned red, and Trisha's hand rose out of the water. When her face appeared, she let out a throat-ripping scream.

Ray's body stiffened. He jumped into the blood-stained sea for Anna's cousin. Trisha, hysterical, smacked his face as she fought for the rope ladder.

As he pushed her to the boat, he asked, "What was it?"

Frantic, she didn't answer. He didn't blame her and had to ignore what could be below him so he could make sure she made it safely aboard.

Willie and Anna reached down for her as Ray stabilized her on the ladder. Her legs dangled in front of him. Blood poured out of her calf and shreds of skin hung off bare bone. A chunk of muscle slipped out of her leg and plopped into the water.

Ray gagged as he stared at the wound. His heart racing, he spun around, searching for whatever had attacked her, searching the splashing surface. He yelled,

"Hurry up and get her on! Something is down here."

Once Trisha was tugged onboard, Anna rushed to the rope ladder and knelt down for Ray. Her eyes froze, lips trembled, and the look on her face sent his pulse racing.

She screamed, "*SHARK.*"

Ray spun in the water, just in time to see a massive shadow glide right at him, parallel to the side of the sailboat.

Roaring, he thrust himself off the ladder. The shark darted between him and the boat. He felt it graze his leg but it didn't bite him.

He almost cheered out loud, *Missed me, you fucking fish!*

Anna, standing near the edge of the boat, watched as the shark swam away. Ray caught a glimpse of its fin before it went under. He didn't bother looking underwater, and threw his body at the boat.

"Swim!" Anna screamed several times.

Water chopped at his face. He was about five feet from the ladder, and he swung his arms and kicked his legs, racing to get back to her. The sea smacked his ears. Some of his other friends yelled at him to hurry, but he couldn't make out their voices.

When he reached the ladder, he fought to climb up as he stared at Anna and asked, "Where is it?"

"I don't know. Just get out."

"I am."

"Come on."

"Where is it?"

"I don't know. I… Ray!"

He saw the white mouth opening for him, but he knew Anna would get him first.

Knife-edged teeth sank into his legs. He was yanked right out of Anna's hold but grabbed the ladder. His palms ripped against the rope.

Anna was close, so close Ray thought he'd hold her

hand.

For her touch always calmed him.

He was gone, leaving her with only bubbles and blood.

Anna collapsed forward, trying to touch him, knowing he'd come back to her.

She knew it.

Willie grabbed her before she jumped off the boat. Tears fell from her eyes and dropped into the ocean to find her Ray. She called out his name, and would keep calling until he—

A hand suddenly rose from the bloody depths and grabbed the ladder. Ray pulled himself up, his eyes wider than Anna had ever seen them.

She reached for him, and their hands were only inches apart, and she needed to feel his touch at least one more time.

The massive shark darted right into Ray's back, slamming him against the sailboat. His blood ejected across Anna's face. She fell hard on her side. Pain struck her throat and chest. When she scrambled back to the ladder, her eyes had to be playing a cruel trick on her because a shark did not just kill Ray. *A shark did not just kill Ray.*

Red water splashed lightly against the boat.

Del had been fast asleep until screams woke him. He'd hoped the screams were fake since he was having the sweetest of dreams about finishing med school and celebrating with his friends Ray and Zeke. They clanked their beers together, and everyone was smiling, and the three-prong power plug was never happier. Del felt pride for the first time in a long time.

In the dream, Zeke had said, "To the Triple P."

"And our new doctor," Ray had added. "Dr. Delford."

Del had laughed at that. There was so much joy, so much joy in a dream.

Flying out of the interior of the sailboat, Del reached Vicki, who was on her knees and covering her mouth. He looked at the others on the main deck. Zeke held the unconscious Trisha, while Willie paced back and forth by the wooden mast, and Anna was frozen at the edge of the boat.

He rushed to her, his breaths rapid as he said, "What happened? Where's Ray?"

A severed arm floated to the surface.

act two

BIO

Beeping. What the hell was that beeping?

Quentin Samuels weakly opened his eyes. His chest burned, his throat tightened, and his head exploded with pain. He yelled at the beeping, "What?"

The marine biologist hopped off the green cushioned bench at the back of his small houseboat. His feet kicked and crushed empty cans of beer, empty plastic bottles of liquor, baggies of leftover weed, and a couple of half-filled bottles of pills.

No way had he used all of those last night. He wasn't even a drinker, but he remembered hoping to drown his sorrows away.

It hadn't worked, and the beeping was trying to rip him in half.

To make matters worse, Quentin hadn't tied his houseboat to the dock. Normally he wouldn't have cared; however, he was out of gas and stranded.

He pressed his hands through his sun-kissed afro, grabbed his head, and said to himself, "I really should have gone solar."

The marine biologist reached into his white cargo shorts and pulled out his cellphone. His finger hovered over the name Alicia. He looked around at sea. The dark blue water was calm, the light blue sky was almost clear, and he could see land and the marina in the short distance.

"Just call her," he told himself. The other line rang a few times before going to voicemail. "Hey, uh." He cleared his throat. "Hey, it's Quentin. If you aren't busy, do you think you could come…." He looked at his sunburnt feet and told himself there were dozens of other people he should be calling instead. "Actually, uh, sorry, never mind. I shouldn't have called. Um, yeah, take care. Bye."

Quentin slipped the phone back into his pocket and shook his head. He fell onto the green cushioned bench and gripped his aching temples. "You're an idiot."

He realized the beeping stopped. What had it been?

An hour vanished before Quentin was towed back to the marina. He anchored his houseboat that time, hopped off the small vessel and onto the wooden dock, which creaked as he walked.

A man taller than him approached, a familiar man who made Quentin want to fill his body with last night's vices. "Great," he muttered as he stared at the large man. He then flashed a big fake smile. "How's it going, Eli? Hunting some sharks today?"

Elijah Augustus paused in front of Quentin and stared him down. His mane of brown hair fluttered in the wind. His eyes widened. "What's it to you?"

"I just find it amusing your profession is shark hunting." Quentin gazed past Eli, at a shorter man carrying supplies. "Who is he? I thought you hunt alone."

Eli didn't break his stare from Quentin. "That would be Dickens, my trusty assistant."

"What's up, buddy?" Quentin said.

Dickens didn't respond. He was a short, pudgy man with a dirt-covered face and wore a red trill fishing hat coated in stains, and was slightly older than the other two men.

Quentin looked back at Eli. "What's his problem?"

"Dickens is deaf."

"Oh."

"He is also blind, mute and partially retarded."

No words could leave Quentin because he believed Eli was messing with him. Still, he didn't want to be rude, so he just stayed silent.

Eli pushed past the marine biologist. "Have a nice one there, Quenty."

Dickens strutted past the marine biologist and followed Eli to the end of the dock.

Before leaving last night's mistakes on his boat, Quentin glanced back at the shark hunter and his companion and yelled at them, "What are you hunting today, Eli?"

Eli's mane of hair blew as quickly as his voice. "The great white."

Quentin groaned and hated himself for not leaving, but as hungover as he was, he hated shark hunters even more. "Let me guess," he said. "The one that killed the vet? Or the one that ate the Billings kid?"

"Same shark. Same beast."

"No. Sharks have not developed a taste for human flesh. They won't be around here. I know the way you think, Eli. We have gone through all of this before. Sharks don't like the taste of us."

His eyes bulging from their sockets, Eli shoved his face an inch from Quentin's nose. "Listen to me, you backstabbing wallabacker! You don't know shit."

"Walla-what?"

Eli pulled away from him, tucked in his lower lip, chewed on it for a second, then turned and hocked a clump of spit into the dark sea where it floated atop calm water. He didn't acknowledge Quentin after that, motioning for Dickens to board the fishing vessel.

Quentin shook his head. "Fine. I'm telling you, you are wasting your time."

The two men sailed away.

Scratching the back of his hairy neck, Quentin stared at his reflection in the water. He wondered why Eli was still holding a grudge against him after all that time. Maybe the man was just that stubborn, or maybe he—

Phlegm floating over his reflection cut off his thoughts.

A phone call followed, one from Alicia. He answered, "Hey. Listen, sorry I—"

"Quentin," she said quickly with concern, "I need to see you now."

"Alicia? What is it?"

"Now!"

PI

THREE HOURS EARLIER....

A bell rang as the door opened to the stuffy office. On the door was a crooked sign reading ALVAREZ: PI.

Kathy Billings breathed deeply as she stepped toward the receptionist's desk. It was empty. *This is a mess*, she thought. Books and papers were all over the place, some half-full glasses of water too. *Does Ms. Alvarez get business anymore?*

Then a raspy mumbled voice said from a different room, "One moment."

Kathy's hand tightened around her briefcase. She considered she should go to someone else.

A Latin woman in her mid-thirties peeked out from the other room. She was short and slender with spiked black hair on her tan head. She raised a thin dark eyebrow as if surprised to see someone there. "Can I help you?"

Kathy Billings nodded. "Yes, I believe you can."

Alicia circled around her large, mahogany desk. She didn't have many things in her life she was proud of, but she loved that damned desk. "Welcome to Alvarez: PI," she said to the woman. Dropping into a black leather chair, Alicia rested her arms in her lap and crossed her legs. She gave the woman a strong and confident stare. "How can I help you?"

"Ms. Alvarez—"

"Please call me Alicia."

"Alicia. My name is Kathy Billings, and I need your help."

"Tell me."

"About a week ago, uh, my two boys were out kayaking off the coast right here." Kathy lowered her head. "My eldest, Sebastian, he was attacked and killed by a shark."

"My deepest sympathies."

"Thanks," sighed Kathy. "My youngest, Billy, he was there. He made it. But he's been traumatized ever since." She sniffled and raised a hand to her face. "Excuse me." She fumbled in her purse, but Alicia was already extending a tissue to her.

"Thanks." She wiped her nose and eyes. "Ms. Alvarez, I mean Alicia, this might be an uncommon request, but I want you to find and kill the shark that ate my boy."

Alicia tried to keep a straight face but wheezed. "I'm sorry. What? I don't know the first thing about finding a shark." She reached into her drawer and pulled out a large cigar.

The woman lifted a briefcase. "Yes, but you find things, Alicia. You have the resources. I don't care if you have outside help. I am willing to pay generously."

Alicia held the unlit cigar in one hand and waved her other. "Kathy, I'm sorry about your boys, I really am. But I can't accept."

Kathy opened the briefcase, revealing stacks of $100 bills.

Alicia's jaw dropped. She reached into her drawer again and pulled out a lighter. "Do you mind?"

"No. I like to smoke mine on Sundays."

"Amen." Alicia smiled as she lit up the Cuban cigar and pressed her thick lips around it. "Tell me something, Kathy. How much money is in that pretty briefcase of yours?"

"A million."

A puff of smoke ejected out of Alicia's mouth, followed by several coughs. She slammed a hand on the desk as she choked.

"Are you okay?"

Alicia's watering eyes stared in disbelief at that crazy woman. "Hell, for a million dollars, darling, I'll filet the fish myself."

Kathy didn't seem amused, but she pushed the briefcase at the private investigator. "I want that shark killed." She rose to her feet. "And I want its head. This is half the money. You get the other half when you get that fish who ate my son and bring me proof it's dead."

"500k now, 500 after?" Alicia asked as she reached for the briefcase. "Works for me."

"You misunderstand. A million now. A million when you kill the shark."

Alicia had been in the shitter before, but it seemed she'd just earned her retirement.

In the doorway, Kathy said, "Ms. Alvarez, I am a very powerful woman in Solana Beach. Don't run off with this money. Understand?"

"Don't worry, Mrs. Billings." She rose from behind her desk. "That shark died the moment you walked into this office."

Alicia pulled up to a coffee shop in her jeep and hopped out upon turning off the engine. She sprinted over to the plastic table where Quentin Samuels was sitting. An umbrella covered him in shade; palm trees danced in the wind and the area was pretty much empty, save for a few other people inside the shop.

"Whoa! Whoa!" Quentin stood as she crashed into the plastic table after tripping over herself while sprinting. He ran to her side to help her, but she waved him off.

The two regained themselves and sat at the green table.

"I can't believe any of this." Alicia smiled in disbelief.

"So she's giving you a million to kill a shark? You don't know the first thing about killing sharks, babe. What is she? Nuts?"

"I don't care if she's the kookiest crackpot in Cali. We have to find that shark."

"We?"

"Well, yeah. I need your help. You know a lot about sharks, and you know that shark hunter guy, right? What's his name?"

Quentin groaned, "Elijah."

"Yeah, him. We need him."

Rubbing the scruff on his face, he looked like he had one shitty night. "I thought you want nothing to do with me?"

"Quentin! This is a lot of money we are talking about. We can put our romantic differences aside for the next few days, right?"

"You messed me over pretty good, Alicia. You should've seen me last night. I'm still not over—"

"You know what? I'll easily find him myself if you are going to be a—"

Quentin grabbed her. "Sorry. Sorry. For that much money, I can forget our past."

"Good. I think this will help us both feel better."

He only shrugged.

There was an awkward tension between them, and to get rid of it, she said, "Let's get Eli now?"

"No."

Alicia dug the toughness in his answer. "No?"

"We don't need him."

"But I thought he was a shark hunter."

"A shark hunter isn't a real thing. He just claims to be one."

"Well, he hunts sharks?"

"Yes."

"So then that makes him a shark hunter."

"*No*, that would make him an idiot. He thinks sharks are like vicious man-eaters from the movies. Sharks couldn't care less about us. We are more dangerous to them than they are to…."

Alicia stared at the table for a few seconds, blocking out Quentin's voice, waiting for him to finish his rant. She'd heard that rant plenty of times before, and when his lips were no longer moving, she asked if he was done.

"Yeah. I'm done."

"Just answer me this. Is he good at finding sharks?"

Quentin placed his hand on his cheek as he leaned to the side. "He's the best guy I know at finding sharks. There is something about him that attracts the fish, I guess. I don't know. It's crazy. Actually, you know what? I saw him earlier today. He was going out to find the great white that killed that vet."

"Same one that killed the Billings boy?"

"Highly unlikely. A number of juvenile whites have been tracked migrating down to Baja from Northern waters. Could have been any one of them passing through."

"But not the same one?" Alicia blinked rapidly under her bug-eyed sunglasses. She knew she was embarking on the most exciting case of her career. "We need the one that killed the kid. How will she prove we killed the right shark? I don't know. But if the shark that killed the vet is the same one that killed the kid, well, shit, seems like we will be doing this world a favor."

"Same one? I doubt it. Sharks don't like the taste of us. Usually an attack is because they mistake us for a seal or are just curious."

"Yeah, that's basic shark 101."

"Hey, you asked, and I'm giving you an answer."

"Relax, Quentin, just screwing with you. You're too serious sometimes."

"Yeah, well, fine." He looked away. "How are we splitting that money?"

Alicia stood. "You and me take forty each and we give the other 20 percent to Eli if we decide to use him."

"Okay." Quentin threw on his aviators. "Let's get rich."

WOUNDS

Within thick fog, the sailboat containing the six remaining friends bobbed up and down. Not even ten minutes had passed since Ray met his fate.

Zeke, Del, and Willie stood around Trisha. Unconscious on a berth in the cabin, she seemed dead, and Zeke had to fight from looking at the bite wound in her calf.

Del pulled off his red shirt, revealing his ripped torso and chest. He then spun around in place, searching for something.

"What do you need?" Willie asked.

"I was only in med school for two years so give me a second." Del spotted soap by the galley sink, shot a hand over and grabbed it. "Get a glass of water."

Willie swung his head around. Unable to find any glasses, he gripped a near empty bottle of beer. He stuck it under the sink faucet and filled.

Meanwhile, Del poured soap onto Trisha's bite wound. The back of her pale calf hung open. Pieces of flesh dangled around the hole revealing bone and muscle. She suddenly jolted awake and screamed in pain as the soap oozed into her torn open skin.

"The water!" Del called back to Willie.

Willie rushed the bottle of water to him. After splashing the wound, Del tied his red shirt around

Trisha's torn leg. Her painful cries continued. Willie grabbed her hand.

While they worked to save Trisha, Zeke stepped back for the ladder. He didn't want to be down there with her, *hated being down there with her*, but he also needed to explain to his friends that he'd accidentally pushed her in the water.

I didn't want anything bad to happen to her.

Trisha's screams sent him fleeing to the main deck.

Light rays of sun fought to break through the dense fog of the late morning sky. A cool breeze crept around the sailboat.

Vicki sat with the frozen Anna, holding her only a few feet from the edge of the boat where the rope ladder hung, where Ray had fought to climb aboard before being devoured by the massive shark. She'd never seen so much blood before, and ripped open flesh, and screaming and crying. Her stomach quivered as she thought about Ray's last moments.

To ease her mind, she focused on Anna and rubbed her hand through her friend's strawberry-blonde hair. "It's going to be okay," she whispered. "I promise."

Vicki didn't believe herself.

She looked over at Zeke, who was bent over grabbing his knees, and waved for him to come over.

Hesitant in his approach, he asked in an irritated tone, "What?"

"How is Trisha?"

"I don't know. I didn't mean to…."

Vicki turned away and lowered her cheek onto Anna's head, ignoring his excuses. She didn't regret being with him the night before but she did find his reaction to Trisha disgusting.

"What are we going to do?" Zeke asked. "Holy fuck, Ray is dead. What are we going to do?"

"We have to get back to shore," Anna said.

"You know how to drive this thing?"

She nodded slightly. "I need the ignition key. Ray left it in the galley."

"Hell yes, Anna." A fat smile filled Zeke's lips. "I'll go get it. Hang on." He spun around and rushed to the cabin, flinging himself legs first through the square interior entrance.

Vicki said to Anna, "Everything will be okay."

"I just don't want to think about it now." She sniffled, moved away from her friend, leaned on one arm, and stared at her. "I know you hate Trisha but promise me we don't lose her."

Vicki fought back tears, touched Anna's hand, and said, "I don't hate her. I... whatever it takes, Anna. Whatever you want, babe. I'm here."

Anna wiped her face, and when she smiled, it seemed incredibly forced like she was using it to keep herself from breaking down.

I'm used to her being the strong one, Vick thought. *I can't see her like this. I can't.*

As Del kept pressure on Trisha's leg, Zeke flew into the cabin and asked for the ignition key. Willie reached passed him and grabbed the key hanging in plain sight off a small hook next to the stove.

"There you go," Willie said and then joined Del.

Zeke looked so lost, Del almost felt bad for him. He could tell his friend wanted to say something, maybe even apologize, but Zeke did his usual thing and left. Del's first instinct was to follow his friend and support him. However, he knew he couldn't leave Trisha.

"I hate this," Willie said.

"You said sharks don't like the taste of us?"

"Yeah."

Saliva sprayed off Del's lips. "Bullshit."

"From what I know, sharks usually take a bite out of us, realize they don't like the taste, swim off... I know that, and I'm pretty sure they're able to swim backward."

"Sharks can't swim backward," Del said with confidence.

"They did in *Deep Blue Sea*."

"That's a movie about genetically engineered sharks."

"You're a movie about genetically engineered sharks!"

"Okay, Willie. Just forget that nonsense for a second. You said they take one bite and swim off, and I agree with you on that, but this one attacked Trisha, then Ray."

"Yeah." Willie lowered his eyes. "It attacked Ray once. Then came back for the damn kill."

"It's hunting us," Del said, his scalp prickling at the notion.

"No. *No*." Willie seemed unsure of himself. "I mean it can't be, right?"

A girl screamed from the main deck, "Shark!"

GO

Anna leaned away from the edge of the boat, trying to block out the sounds of Ray's pain.

He was gone, and there was nothing she could do except get Trisha back to shore. *You died saving her, Ray. I'll make sure it wasn't for nothing.*

Zeke climbed out of the interior of the sailboat with the ignition key in hand.

"Are you ready?" Vicki asked Anna. "We can wait if you want. We don't have to move."

Anna stood. "We need to get Trisha to the hospital. I don't want to wait. Ray wouldn't want us to wait."

Vicki kissed her friend's head then squinted past her. "Anna," she whispered. "Anna, what is that?"

A dark speck sliced through the water in the distance. When it got closer, the dorsal fin accelerated, heading straight for the boat.

Anna backed away from the ledge as Vicki screamed, "Shark!"

"Holy shit," Zeke said. "Look at the size of it!"

Anna had already seen how large it was, right before it killed Ray. She didn't need to see it again, but she knew it would haunt her for the rest of her life.

"What is it doing?" Vicki asked Zeke.

"Hopefully apologizing," he said as he moved toward the interior of the boat where Willie rushed out of.

Looking overboard, Willie gasped. "It's coming for us. Why is it coming for us?"

For a moment, everyone stayed still and silent.

Anna came to her senses and held out her hands and demanded Zeke to throw her the ignition key.

He tossed it to her then dove past Del and into the cabin of the boat. "*Fucking sharks*," he yelled.

As Anna ran for the upper deck, Willie told everyone to grab onto something. He pulled Vicki toward the middle mast. Vicki tried to grab Anna, but Anna wasn't stopping for anyone or anything.

She would get the motor on. She would get them back to land.

Holding the interior entrance, Del reached for Anna and said, "Grab my hand."

Sorry, Del. Not for you. Not for anyone. She was halfway up the ladder leading to the cockpit when the shark struck the sailboat.

A jolting shock rumbled through the wooden hull, causing the boat to spin. Anna lost her footing and was thrown off the ladder. She slammed onto the main deck. Pain engulfed her lower back. She saw Del reaching for her but he was knocked into the interior, vanishing before her eyes.

She screamed, knowing she was about to fall overboard.

Somehow she got one hand on the rope lifeline surrounding the sides of the boat, preventing her from hitting the water. In her other hand was the ignition key.

She didn't have a strong grip on the rope, her toes were just inches above the surface of the ocean, and she saw flashes of Ray as he was killed by the shark.

Her fingers slid, the rope burning her skin.

She told herself to swim straight for the ladder once she hit the water, then eased her hand and fell.

Someone grabbed her wrist.

Arms and face sliding off the edge of the boat, Willie's chubby body was about to plummet into the sea with Anna. His first thought had been, *Holy crap I caught her!* Then it turned to, *Holy crap I'm going in the water!*

Someone slammed down on his back. Delford. He hugged Willie's stomach, anchoring him. Del clenched his teeth as he yelled, "Don't you let go of her!"

Willie hung over the boat's edge, while Anna squirmed around in the water, and he yelled, "Pull us up!"

"Nah," Del said, "I thought we'd all hang here for a while." Then he spat, "The hell you think I'm doing, man?"

Willie looked into Anna's terrified eyes. "I got you. Don't worry, I got you."

She nodded, her lips quivering.

Her body, along with Willie, began to rise. When he made it back on the boat, her legs were pulled out of the water, and she kicked in midair as half her body made it aboard.

Willie realized Zeke was helping Del and thought, *He's not totally useless.*

Almost fully on the boat, Anna managed to smile at Willie.

"Swing your legs up," he said.

Although he couldn't see below her, he heard a thunderous splash.

Anna's smile vanished.

Willie, still holding onto her, was tugged face first over the edge of the boat. He stared at Anna's legs in the large mouth of the shark. Its dark gray top disappeared below the surface before he could get a better view of it. Water splashed around its face. Blood poured into the white ocean.

Anna's wide and teary eyes stared at Willie. He screamed with all his might, fighting to get her back.

I got you, I so got you.

The shark widened its mouth, launched up, and chomped into Anna's stomach.

Blood spilled down the sides of her cheeks and neck, and her face shook as she gurgled at Willie to save her.

"Pull us up," he screamed at the guys. "Fucking pull us up!"

They did, but only half of Anna made it with him.

JACKETS

"Where are we going, Quentin? That was the exit for the docks."

Quentin drove Alicia's jeep on a near empty freeway. Without looking at her, he said, "I want to go to the coroner first."

"Coroner?"

"Yeah, my friend Eric works there. He still has the bodies of the Billings kid and the vet."

"We know they were killed by sharks. What is the point of this?"

"You'll see." Although he did his best to focus on the task at hand, Quentin wanted to grab Alicia's hand, kiss it, and have her fall in love with him again. But he refrained because she would likely slap him if he touched her.

Palm trees flew past as they sped off the next exit. When they arrived to their destination, the coroner Eric Herring greeted them with a large smile. "Always a pleasure to see you, Mr. Samuels."

Quentin snuck a handful of cash to Eric.

"Right this way," said the coroner.

Alicia laughed and followed the two men.

Two bodies were already set out on tables for them, both zipped up in bags.

"The boy is here," Eric said. "The vet there. I should

warn you two this won't be pretty."

"Shark attacks usually aren't." Quentin pulled out a pair of thick-framed glasses as he unzipped the bag to see the body of Sebastian Billings.

Alicia gagged and turned around. "This is all you, Quentin."

The marine biologist kept quiet to himself for several minutes before looking over at the coroner. He wouldn't admit what he was thinking, at least not yet. "It was determined already both attacks were done by a great white?"

"Indeed."

Searching for the right thought to voice, he looked up at the ceiling. "You know, not too long ago, several years I believe, a swimmer was killed by a great white around the same location as these two."

Eric scratched his face. "Makes sense the attacks are all in the same area."

"How's that?" Quentin was half listening to Eric as he stared at Sebastian's dead face. The kid looked at peace.

"Well, right off Solana Beach, near the cove, it's a popular place for swimmers, kayakers, divers. Hell, if it's a water sport, probably done over there."

"Doesn't explain why a white is over there eating people."

Alicia mumbled, "Lots of people equals lots of food."

"No. Like I've always said, great whites only attack us 'cause they think we're a seal or some other mammal. They don't like the taste of us, which is why most deaths are from one fatal wound." He looked up from the body of the vet and at Alicia. "After one bite, it realizes it made a mistake and swims off."

"How many times are you going to say that?" she asked.

The coroner interrupted them. "You say it realizes after one bite? The vet has two."

Quentin removed his glasses. "Which raises the question: why is this shark attacking humans?"

Alicia pointed back and forth at the bodies, trying not to breathe. "Both corpses, uh, same shark?"

After folding his glasses into his pocket, Quentin scratched his head, despising the words on the tip of his tongue.

"What is it?" Alicia asked.

"The bite patterns are exactly the same on both bodies. Unfortunately, I was wrong. It is one shark."

"Great," mumbled Alicia.

"Yeah. I hate to say it, but you're right. We need Elijah Augustus."

They left to find their shark hunter.

"I want one coffee cup, full of your worst gin. Then give me a clear glass full of your best vodka. Then I want—"

"Sir." The waitress cleared her throat. "This is a family diner. We don't serve hard liquor here."

From the red booth, Elijah Augustus stared at the waitress as if he were looking at an alien from another planet. He then looked at his loyal companion, his brown mane of hair fluttering in the process. "Where have you taken me, Dickens?"

Dickens—the deaf, blind, mute and partially retarded comrade of the shark hunter—was busy fumbling with a fork and staring up at the ceiling.

"Sir, when you two are ready, wave me down."

Eli continued to stare at the pudgy Dickens, his hand rolling into a fist. After a few seconds, Eli released a long exhale. "I can never stay mad at you." He called back for the waitress. "I shall have a glass of milk!"

Just then, the diner door rang open. Quentin Samuels stepped inside from the night. Some pretty princess followed him.

Eli cocked his head hard. "Well, well. Quenty needs

the help of a real man. Teach him how to tug his dick the right way, ay?"

Quentin stopped a few feet short of the C-shaped booth and looked at his pretty princess. "Do we really have to do this?"

The woman shoved past him. "Eli, my name is Alicia Alvarez. Thanks for meeting us."

Eli was still looking at Quentin, smiling with pride, and when he finally turned to Alicia, he stared directly at her crotch just to see what she was made of.

She didn't budge.

Eli, not averting his eyes, said, "What can I do you for, Niagara Falls?"

Alicia thrust a hand around a fork next to Eli's arm, lifted it up and stabbed it down onto the table. "Listen, asshole, and listen well. You either shut up and help us or screw off."

"My, oh my. You are a salty pretzel, aren't you?"

She sighed and turned to Quentin. "Maybe we should leave."

Eli chuckled. "Enough paddy-cake playing around. I'll help you two out. I'll find your shark. I'll kill your shark." He slapped Quentin on the butt. "And for a free bonus, I'll teach Quenty how to use that spaghetti noodle he calls his penis."

Alicia and Eli shook hands on it.

"All right," groaned Quentin. "So what's your plan?"

"Oh, you are hysterical." Laughing, the shark hunter tried to tickle Quentin, but the silly man-boy jumped away. "We don't need a plan. We need our wits. We need a boat. We need the ocean. We need—"

Quentin yelled, "*Enough.*"

All the patrons looked at their table.

Eli rose and met each one of their eyes with the confidence of a thousand gorillas as he said, "Listen to me, boy and girl. This aquatic beast isn't messing around, and neither am I. So you all better tighten your death jackets because we leave at sunrise."

Both Alicia and Quentin looked confused, which wasn't the reaction Eli had been expecting after saying that epic liner.

"They're called life jackets," Alicia said.

"Huh?" Eli asked.

"You said death jackets. They're not called death jackets. They're called life jackets because they preserve life."

"Then why do people die in them?"

Alicia groaned and looked at Quentin. "Is he always like this?"

"Yep."

Not wanting to waste any more time, Elijah Augustus grabbed both their shoulders and gave them a line for the ages: "Let's go fishing."

LEFT

On the upper deck of the sailboat, Zeke wrapped his arm around Vicki. She wasn't crying as she rocked back and forth, and Zeke found her silence worse than sobs. He comforted her the best he could, sighing as he stared out at the gray sky.

Fog floated around them. Land was nowhere to be seen.

Zeke had no clue where they were.

"What are we going to do?" Vicki whispered.

How would he know? One of his best friends was dead. Now Anna. He said to her, "We just stay out of the water."

"No shit."

On the white wood of the main deck, streams of blood ran out of Anna's ripped-open torso. Del was closest to her, while Willie sat against the middle mast of the boat.

"Tell me something," Willie said, his face in his hands. "Does Anna still have the ignition key?"

Zeke had forgotten about the key, and the thought of it brought him some hope.

Then Del said, "No. Her palms are empty."

Willie breathed heavily. "Then, I think it's best we dispose of the body."

"I guess. Yes."

Bumping into Zeke as she grabbed the railing on the upper deck, Vicki said to the guys below, "You aren't serious? She is not going back in the water."

On his feet and stepping next to the short ladder leading up to her, Willie said, "I hate it, too. But you want blood to keep dripping off this boat, giving that shark more desire to eat the rest of us?"

She laughed and threw up her hands. "I don't believe this." She turned to Zeke. "Tell them they're wrong."

Looking down at Willie and Del, then at the rest of Anna's body and back at Vicki, Zeke said, "I think you're wrong."

She grunted and shoved him. "Go sit down there with them. I need to be alone."

"Whatever, dude. I don't care."

She slapped him.

"You're a terrible kisser," he said.

She slapped him again.

"*Enough*," Del demanded as he stood over Anna's body. "Willie. Zeke. Meet me inside."

Something in Vicki's eyes told Zeke to get the hell out of there, so he followed the guys into the cabin of the boat.

They drew straws for who would tip Anna's body overboard.

Zeke pulled the shortest.

Of course it was him. Everything was his fault, right? Had he never pushed Trisha into the water then maybe everyone would still be alive.

"I didn't mean to do it," he told Willie and Del. "I didn't mean to push her off."

"You're not getting out of this," Willie said.

"I know."

Out on the main deck, Zeke looked at Anna's body. Well, half of it. Pieces of skin hung loosely off her abdomen where meat and bone had dripped out. Her

90

skin was a dead white, and her eyes were still frozen open.

Her eyes stared up at Zeke like they wanted to tell him something.

He covered his mouth and gagged at the grisly sight, hoping he'd wake up soon from that nightmare, or for it to turn into some awesome sex dream.

Crouched by the corpse, his hands shook as he grabbed cold dead shoulders. He dragged the body but lost his footing. His face smashed into something wet. When he touched his cheek, he realized Anna's blood was sticking to his skin and fingers. He scrambled to his feet, rushed to the edge of the boat and heaved.

Nothing came out.

Realizing his toes were hanging over the ledge, Zeke flung back and flailed toward the cabin.

The shark wasn't getting him. No way was the shark gonna get him.

On his butt near the body, he breathed deeply. "Just do it. *Nike*."

He marched to Anna, knelt over her, and found himself saying, "I hope you're with Ray."

After shoving her into the water, Zeke knew Ray and Anna were in fact together. Because if they weren't together in another life, they were surely together in the stomach of the shark.

Del stood over Trisha, applying pressure to her leg wound. She remained unconscious. As he looked at her, the walls of the cabin closed in, telling him he better not let her die or his world would be over. His lips moved but he didn't hear himself say to the other guys, "We need to get her to a hospital."

Willie stared at the floor, sitting on the berth alone. "I had her. I had Anna in my hands."

At the tiny table, Zeke said, "Don't do it, Willie."

"Do what?"

"Feel sorry for anything. You did what you could have."

"Oh yeah? And what did you do?" Willie jumped to his feet. "If you didn't shove Trisha into the water…." He looked like he regretted saying as much as he did.

Zeke marched right to him. "Finish that sentence, William. What would have happened?"

"You know damn right what would—"

"Enough!" Del stepped between them, his nostrils flaring. "This is not the time to blame each other."

Willie sighed and backed away. "You're right. I just don't get why the shark is doing this. Why the hell does it want us dead?"

Turning away from the others, Zeke grunted. "Maybe it's done. But we need to forget about the shark for now. It can't get us if we stay away from the water. So what we need to do is figure out how to get back to land."

Del smiled. He wasn't sure why. "Simple enough. We sail back?"

"Well great, Delford! Do you know one thing about sailing? 'Cause Willie and I sure as hell don't. And I'm going to make a wild assumption here, but Vicki doesn't know either, and Trisha sure as shit can't do anything right now."

Del lowered his head. "I don't know how to sail."

"Awesome. So that's out. Now what?"

"We call for help. Who's got a cell phone?" Willie asked.

Del sighed. "I didn't think I'd need one."

"Zeke?"

"I, uh, I wanted to avoid my ex so I didn't bring one."

Willie said, "Gotcha."

"What about you?" Zeke asked like he was accusing

Willie of something.

Willie lowered his fat face. "I didn't charge it before we left. It's dead."

"Un-fucking-believable. Not one phone?"

Del shrugged. "Probably wouldn't get service out here anyway."

Letting out a breath like all hope was lost, Willie said, "There are really only two options left." The others looked at him, waiting for him to continue. He said, "We sit here and wait for someone to find us, or…."

Zeke lowered his head to meet Willie's eyes. "*Or what?*"

"We swim."

Obnoxious laughs flew out of Zeke's mouth. "You aren't serious?"

"As a last resort. The swim to land is doable. We can't be out that far."

Del knew Zeke was in disbelief, and for once, he had to agree with his friend.

"I'm going to see if Vicki has her phone," Zeke said then pointed at Willie. "Don't even think about going in the water. This boat is the one advantage we have over the shark. The only one." He climbed up the ladder and was gone.

Willie grunted as he looked over at Del. "What do you think?"

Standing in the galley, he said, "We got three bottles of water left and a couple of slices of bread. Oh, and some string cheese. I guess when the time comes, we need to ask ourselves something."

"What's that?"

"Would we rather risk starvation and dehydration. Or risk being ripped apart by that shark?"

Willie gulped. "I didn't even think about starving. But we're far from that, right?"

"Yeah, I think so." Del second-guessed himself

because after losing Ray and Anna, he figured unlikely terrible things could happen at any time.

"So then the real question we have to ask ourselves is this." Willie stood next to Del, both of them looking at Trisha. "How long can we keep her alive before we have to swim for help?"

WAITING

Regardless of the nasty stare Vicki was giving Zeke, he wanted to reach land and would do anything to get there, even if it meant begging Vicki for her phone.

Luckily she didn't give him any lip and said, "It's in my duffle bag."

Zeke smiled, didn't see the duffle bag up there, and turned back for the ladder that led to the main deck.

Vicki whispered, "Hey."

"Yeah?"

"Can you send Willie up here?"

Looking at the floor, he muttered, "Sure thing."

"We shouldn't have been together last night."

"I know." He was glad she wanted Willie with her because he wasn't cut out for comforting a girl, not after his heart had been smashed by his ex. Plus her request should make Willie somewhat happy.

In the interior, Zeke said to his friend, "Vicki wants you up there."

The slouching Willie straightened. "Really? What did she say?"

"She says she wants you up there. Now where's her bag? She has her cell phone."

Willie pointed at a little yellow duffle bag. "I think it's that one." He stood up and climbed to the main deck.

Zeke ripped the bag open, shuffled around a few

articles of clothing and pulled out a small silver phone. "Jackpot!"

Del clapped his hands. "Tell me it has service."

"Two bars, but, shit."

"Don't tell me, Zeke. Don't say it."

"3% power."

"Shit," spat Del. "So who we going to call?"

"The fucking Ghostbusters, Delford." Zeke groaned and dialed 911.

"Sorry, I'm just out of it."

Ignoring him, Zeke raised the phone to his ear. "It's ringing.... Hey, yeah.... Hello?" He looked down at the phone. "Shit." He rushed to the ladder and climbed out of the interior. "Hey? Can you hear me?"

The screen of the phone shut off, turning black.

"Shit!"

In a fury, Zeke threw the phone down on the deck. It bounced a couple of times before flying overboard. He dropped to his knees and knew it was the beginning of the end for him and his friends.

"Dude, what happened?" Del asked.

"It died. *It died.*"

From the upper deck, Vicki said, "Just turn it back on. It usually lasts for like five minutes. Plus I have my charger inside."

No, no, NO. She didn't just say that. How could she just say that? Zeke almost broke into tears as he said, "I... uh...."

Vicki's eyes widened. "You didn't."

"I thought it was dead! I didn't mean for it to fly into the water."

Del threw up his hands. "Dammit! Give us one break, *one break*!" He vanished into the cabin.

Still on his knees, slumped in defeat, Zeke stared at the edge of the boat, realizing how quickly hope was slipping away.

Vicki turned around and sighed. "He better pay me for that."

"I think we have bigger problems to worry about right now." Willie frowned as he sat next to her, and she smelled surprisingly delightful. Sensual, even.

"Yeah, you're right."

"So what's up?" he asked as he looked at the gray sky, realizing Zeke was correct about not being able to see land. *Swimming is a dumb idea. My oops.*

Vicki touched his thigh. "I'm sorry about last night. I was drunk, and I shouldn't have been with Zeke. I mean, it's not like we did much, but I just, I know you were into me and all. I'm not used to nice guys, and Zeke is a gutless jerk. I saw you try to save Anna. And he did nothing. You were very brave."

Willie let out a short laugh. "Like I said, Vicki, bigger problems right now."

"Okay, well, I just want you to know I think you're cute and…."

A large dumb smile crossed Willie's lips, but he didn't care because he'd give her every dumb smile he had to give. "Please just stop there." He leaned in, kissed her, and wasn't surprised by the softness of her lips; they had always looked perfect.

They pulled away from each other, and she snuggled into him as he put an arm around her. She said softly in the cutest voice possible, "William?"

"Yeah?"

"You kinda smell like vomit."

His face burned red. "Oops. Sorry."

"It's okay. Better than the smell of an asshole."

Zeke stood alone at the front of the boat, and Willie couldn't help but laugh.

The anchor, still plunged to the ocean depths, held

them in nearly the same place as yesterday, back when everyone was still alive and SNUBA diving.

Zeke looked around for the shark but found no sign of it. He looked around for land but found no sign of it either. He was in a bubble of gray. *We have to be close to land still. It's just the damn fog hiding it from us.*

Spinning around, Zeke looked up at Willie and Vicki cuddling with each other. He was happy for them. Wait, happy? How could he feel any kind of happiness? Ray and Anna were dead.

Maybe he wasn't happy for them; maybe he just didn't care, maybe—

"Shit!" Zeke found himself saying aloud. He didn't check to see if the lovebirds heard him and went straight for the interior.

Lowering himself down the short ladder into the cabin, he asked Del, "We have any beer left?"

Del raised his head from Trisha. "Really?"

"Hey, we are stuck for now, so might as well enjoy ourselves." He popped open a can of semi-warm beer and took a sip. "Aaahh, delicious." He sat across from his friend. "Join me. Have a drink."

"Na, man. I gotta take care of her. Plus, you know you're going to dehydrate yourself?"

Zeke nodded. "Hey, didn't you drop out of med school? Do you even know what you're doing?"

Del's mouth hung open for a brief second before he said, "I have to try."

"Good. You do that. Let me enjoy myself."

"Whatever, man." Del pushed off the berth and stood. "I'm pretty sure I stopped the bleeding. I need to sit outside a while. So you enjoy yourself in here and come get me if she wakes up."

He raised his can of beer to Del. "Cheers, bro."

"Please don't be an idiot, Zeke."

After chugging the beer, he said to himself,

"Wouldn't dream of it." He let out a healthy burp and gave himself a pat on the back.

He wasn't sure why he was irritated with Del. Maybe he wasn't. Maybe he was just mad at the world and taking it out on the other assholes stuck with him.

On the ground by his sunburnt feet, he looked at the five remaining beers, and he crushed the empty can in his hand then grabbed another delicious beverage.

As the young man drank, he stared at Trisha, who still wore the tankini she had on the day before. Her torso was covered by a tank top, which led to a light blue bikini bottom. Her slender legs were outstretched across the berth. A red shirt was tied around her wounded calf.

Glancing away from the girl, Zeke sipped some more beer. His sips turned to chugs. He crushed the empty can and grabbed another beverage.

Sip. Chug. Crush. Sip. Chug. Crush.

Leaning on the berth across from Trisha, staring at his board shorts, Zeke got a familiar tingling. A cursed tingling. A tingling that ended his relationship with his ex.

He shook his head, sipped some more beer, and tried to focus on anything but the tingling.

When he looked at Trisha's bare leg, the tingling got excited. *Very excited.* Her leg was shaped in a way that attracted him, and he wondered what she was like underneath her tankini.

Excited tingles brought him to his feet. He chugged his beer. Holding onto the empty can, he took a seat at the tiny table right next to Trisha, staring at her slender leg. His eyes wandered from her knee to her inner thigh.

His shorts became too tight, and he knew they needed to come off.

As he undid the strings of his shorts to satisfy the tingles, Zeke bounced on his tiptoes.

The reality of what he was doing slapped him across the face.

Where was that reality all the other times? That reality could've saved his relationship with his ex.

"*THE HELL IS WRONG WITH ME?*" Zeke grabbed the empty beer can and threw it across the cabin. "What was I thinking? *Why was I thinking it?*" He knew he had to get away from Trisha before the tingling took him over again, and he rushed for the ladder.

"Wait," she said.

REALITY

Six hours passed since the shark killed Anna.

The sun set amongst the dense fog while the boat bobbed up and down with small waves, and the five remaining friends sat in the interior. Del was by Trisha, who was awake, and he thanked his lucky stars she hadn't died. He even felt a shred of confidence for the first time in what felt like forever.

Willie and Vicki were on the berth across from him and Trisha, while Zeke was drunk and leaning over the small wooden table between the two berths, resting on his legs.

"It's going to be dark soon," Willie stated.

Zeke, tucking his head under his arm, raised his free hand. "And?"

"And we should try and sail the boat back to shore."

Muffled laughs echoed from Zeke's covered face.

Del leaned toward Willie. "Think you can?"

"I'm assuming we just position the sails in the direction we want the wind to push us."

Zeke raised his red face. "Even if we were able to sail this thing, even if we had enough wind to push us back, you all are forgetting one important fact."

"Yeah? And what's that?"

"We can't see land!" Zeke shot out his arms and toppled over.

"True," Willie said, "but we have been anchored this whole time. We only can't see land 'cause of the fog, but land is always in the same place."

"That's literally the stupidest thing I've ever heard."

"The boat has moved around because of the shark," Vicki said. "So land could be any direction."

"See, William?" Pride filled Zeke's voice. "Even your girlfriend agrees with me."

"I wasn't agreeing with anyone."

The room fell silent. Willie tightened his arm around Vicki, while Zeke swayed back and forth as he tried to maintain balance, and Del covered his face with his hands.

Then as if he solved all of their problems, Del said, "The compass. We can use it."

"It's broken," Willie said then sighed. "My oops."

"Shit. And we don't have a flare gun." Del almost called out Zeke for losing the flare gun, but his friend was getting enough shit, so he left it alone.

"Maybe the sky will clear in the morning," Trisha stated weakly to the group. "Maybe we're okay to stay here tonight?"

"Okay to stay here?" Zeke slid his body to face her. "Did you forget you are bleeding to death? Did you forget about the freak fish that wants to eat us?"

"Enough!" Del stood his ground by the wounded girl as he lowered his piece of string cheese. "Trisha is right. We could wait. There has been no sign of the shark, and I know I said we should get her to a hospital, but her wound is okay for now."

Zeke slapped his hands to his own head. "I'm sorry, but the wound is okay? Her fucking calf got ripped off!"

"Okay, dude. Relax."

Slumped against the ladder leading to the main deck, Zeke slurred, "You know. I thought I was going nuts at first, but I can see I'm the only sane one here." He gave

Del, Willie, Vicki, and Trisha one quick glance then headed to the main deck.

Willie chuckled. "Guy is losing it. Needs help."

Del knew once he had a chat with Zeke, his friend would come to his senses, but first he placed a hand on Trisha's shoulder and asked if she were okay.

Dark circles were around her eyes. "I'm trying not to think about it."

"Just hang tough."

She nodded. "Who is going to help Zeke?"

"No one can," Willie said with a laugh. "Maybe we should draw straws."

"I'll check on him in a bit," Del said, taking a seat. "He just needs to cool off."

The drunk Zeke stood under the night sky, wrapping his arms around his chest to keep warm as a breeze swirled around him. He tightened his hand around his beer, stumbled to the front of the boat and leaned over the edge, staring at the dark waters. He whispered, "Where aarrre yooou, sharky shark?"

The black ocean splashed against the boat. A light mist grazed his face.

He giggled to himself, pulled away from the edge, and eventually made it to the upper deck of the sailboat. Plopped behind the wheel and throttle, Zeke fumbled around, searching for a spare key. Then he saw a radio and thought to himself, *Why hasn't anyone tried using this?*

The radio didn't work.

He punched it, his hand cracked, and he cursed the sky for their shitty luck.

Accepting there was nothing he could do to help himself, he leaned back in the captain's chair, closed his eyes, and hoped to travel somewhere else, somewhere nicer. Maybe somewhere with fluffy bunnies, and beautiful babes, and infinite beer, and *no sharks*.

A creak in the wood startled Zeke. He spun around. Del was behind him. "We need to talk."

"What? Can't talk to the lovebirds Willie and Vicki?" He chuckled to himself.

"Seriously, bro. After Ray, well, you're the only person on board I really know now. You, Ray and I, we go back."

"We were a three-prong power plug."

Del pressed a hand against his chest. "The Triple P."

"Feels weird saying it now that Ray is gone."

"Yeah." Del sat on a bench and wiped his face. "Listen. I was thinking about something."

"Yeah? Shoot."

"Swimming for land."

"No, no, no." Zeke growled as he pointed out to sea. "I'd rather die on this boat than get eaten by that crazy fish."

"Just hear me out." He licked his lips. "If we could distract the shark or trap it or—"

"Are you listening to yourself? You don't know the first thing about sharks, do you?"

"Dammit, Zeke!" He lowered his head. "Look, come with me."

Zeke watched Del rise and head for the main deck. "Why?"

"Just come with me."

He didn't want to follow but for some reason, his body stood from the chair and did just that.

At the side of the sailboat, leaning over the edge where Anna was taken, Del pointed at the flippers behind Zeke.

"What are you going to do, Del?"

"Swim for land."

"We haven't even been stranded for a day. Don't be drastic."

"You're wrong. We've been stranded out here since

the beginning."

"What are you talking about?" Zeke watched him put on the flippers. "The beginning? What are you saying, man? What's going on?"

"That shark. It wants us. It's our passageway into the afterlife. It takes us from this world, takes us to be judged."

Zeke knew he was dreaming. He had to be because Del had never talked like that before. *Did the guy finally snap?*

"Wait... what?" Zeke asked. "How much did I drink?"

Right in front of his face, Del said, "So God help me, I'm not ready to leave this world yet. To be judged."

"What has gotten into you?"

Del whipped out a pocketknife from his board shorts. "I appreciate the sacrifice." He struck the knife into Zeke's thigh.

Eyes opened wide, Zeke could feel his veins bulging from his neck. He couldn't believe Del just stabbed him. He tried to scream for help but couldn't even whisper as he stared at the blade in his flesh. A stream of blood squirted out. He dropped his beer and was sad to see it roll off the boat.

Willie, Trisha, and Vicki appeared behind Del. They all pointed at Zeke and laughed, chanting, "Sacrifice! Sacrifice!"

Del threw an uppercut punch at his jaw, knocking him over the edge of the boat.

The fall to the ocean took so long, but the splash came so quick.

Gasping for air, Zeke knew it was no dream.

"Sacrifice! Sacrifice!" they kept chanting from the sailboat.

With reality sinking in, so did panic. Zeke spun around, looking for the dorsal fin. With no visibility came no warning.

He turned back to the sailboat. It was gone. How could it be gone?

Zeke started to hyperventilate. He tried to yell, but his voice wouldn't return, then he spotted his beer floating next to him. He grabbed it and chugged what was left. Only salt water poured into his mouth.

Zeke screamed and threw the can of beer and—

The death-grip stabbed into his midsection. A large mouth pulled him underwater as he banged his fists against sandpapery skin.

Knowing he couldn't beat his way free, he reached for a lifeline. There was nothing to grab except for his empty beer can.

All hope lost, Ezekiel was pulled to the cold depths of the dark sea, right into hell.

SLICES

Shaking, Zeke snapped awake.

He was sprawled out in the captain's chair behind the wheel of the sailboat. Sweat dripped down his face. His heart raced. He leaned forward and took a couple of deep breaths to regain his composure as he said, "Oh, praise you, Jesus, it was just a dream."

The sky was still foggy, but it was morning.

Zeke stumbled to stand and nearly fell over. He grabbed the steering wheel to help regain balance, felt something in his board shorts and pulled out a ziplock bag, which contained several bread crumbs.

"No. Oh no." He realized he ate the rest of the group's bread.

The last of their food.

Stumbling back to the ladder of the upper deck, his legs ached so badly he lost himself. He collided hard against the floor. Sliding off the main deck of the rocking sailboat, Zeke screamed as his feet flew off the edge.

Somehow, he managed to grab the metal ladder. He yanked himself close to it, even hugged it.

In the cabin on the V-berth with Vicki, Willie looked at her as she slept peacefully. They hadn't been intimate last night, which was fine because he was just glad he got to hold her and keep her safe.

Scratching his head, Willie let out a long yawn that told him to go back to sleep. However, things needed to get done, so he scooted off the V-berth.

Vicki glanced up at him and whispered, "Where are you going?"

"Sorry, did I wake you?"

She shook her head.

"First," Willie said, "I'm going to punch Zeke in the face for eating the last slices of our bread. Stupid drunk dick." He scratched his arm. "Second, I'm going to sail us back to land. I don't care about the fog. We need to get home or at the very least sail away from the shark."

"You think it's still out there?"

"What? No. I'm just saying… it's time to go home."

"I like the sound of that."

He leaned down and kissed her on the cheek. "Just rest. Before you know it, we will be having drinks on the beach."

"I can't wait," she whispered as she rolled over.

On one of the side berths, Trisha was sleeping. Motionless. Her face was deathly pale. Next to her, Del slumped over the tiny table, his large body covering almost the entire thing.

Willie poked him.

He jumped. "What's going on?"

"I'm gonna try and get us back to land."

"How long was I out for?"

"Not sure." Willie nodded at Trisha. "Make sure she is okay, then come out and help me. Time to put that useless Ezekiel to work too."

"Be out in a few."

Zeke was holding the ladder leading to the upper deck. He screamed when Willie came up to him and said, "Thanks for eating our food, jackass."

"I don't remember."

"Whatever. It doesn't matter. I'm sailing us back right now." He marched to the large mast in the middle of the main deck and started to untie the main sail when he paused. He knew his eyes were tricking him. They had to be.

There was no way he was looking at a rising dorsal fin.

Willie yelled at Zeke, "Get the anchor up!"

"Anchor? What's going on?"

"Do it, Zeke! It's coming back!" He frantically tried to figure out how to raise the main sail, but he was in over his head. He just knew he had to try.

When he looked at the ocean again, the dorsal fin was gone.

He breathed relief.

Zeke, at the front of the sailboat, looked at Willie and shrugged. "How the fuck do I raise an anchor?" Then he looked overboard and said, "My God."

As he fumbled with the main sail and watched Zeke, Willie's frustration increased each passing second, but he wouldn't give up because he just wanted to get everyone home.

Backing away from the anchor line, Zeke pointed at the water. "I see it. I fucking see it! It's huge."

"That's what she said," came from Willie's mouth, hoping to keep himself calm.

He was surprised Zeke laughed, especially at a time like that.

Then Del emerged from the cabin. "Guys, we got a big problem."

"Yeah and it's coming for us."

"No, man. A different problem. Trisha isn't breathing."

Willie paused his fumbles. "What?"

"She's dead."

Over his slight shock, Zeke sprinted for the anchor.

The shark had swum past the boat, but it turned around and headed right back for them. *Fifteen feet away from us*, guessed Zeke. *It's almost as big as this damned boat.* Then the dorsal fin sank beneath the surface.

Having grabbed the chain rode of the anchor, he leaned over the rocking ledge and asked anyone, "Where did it go?"

Willie yelled, "Zeke! Wait!"

A large wake splashed up to his face. In his hands, the chain rode of the anchor tugged slightly forward. Then it crept outward, moving the front of the boat, causing a loud, slow creaking noise.

Zeke, still holding the chain, looked at Willie. "What is going on?"

"It can't be… it can't be! Run, Zeke. Run!"

The chain rode flew from the hull out of the hawsehole. It constricted around the wooden ship as it passed into the ocean. A piece of wood struck Zeke in the eye. He fell back, right on his ass, and listened as the bow of the ship ripped open.

Lifting a single eyebrow, Zeke stared at the edge of the boat until Willie rushed up to him. His friend touched his face and said, "You're bleeding all over your cheek. Your neck."

Zeke didn't feel any pain but mumbled, "I'm hit."

Grabbing Zeke's shoulder, Willie dragged him toward the entrance of the cabin.

Del reached them. "What the hell?"

"Get inside," Willie said. "Get inside now."

Del was looking over the side of the ship. "Come see this, Willie."

"I don't need to see it. I know what it is and I don't need to see it."

Zeke yanked Willie toward the side of the boat.

His fat friend said, "I hate being right."

The anchor rode was completely ripped out of the wooden sailboat. A long, skinny gash ran from the main deck down to the bottom of the hull.

The ocean poured into the only thing keeping them safe from the shark.

Dug into the sandy bottom of the sea was the anchor. Its chain rode drifted toward dark depths. Beyond it, the great white shark glided in the darkness, pieces of metal chain stuck in its teeth.

act three

FATHER

Fog crept along the docks on the Solana Beach shore.

Standing on the sand, marine biologist Quentin Samuels carried two duffle bags and had a purple backpack slung over his shoulder. He heard a vehicle pull into the cement parking lot behind him.

Dressed in jean shorts, a white tank top, and purple windbreaker, Alicia Alvarez hopped out of her jeep. Her face was stone as she asked, "Where's Eli?"

"Not even a hello?"

"Quentin! How are you, darling?" She smacked his arm, causing him to flinch.

He grabbed her hand. "Hey."

"What?"

"While we're out at sea, maybe we should have a talk?"

"Yeah, maybe."

"Because I really—"

"Hola!" A voice called out from their side. Elijah Augustus approached them wearing a light blue tank top and bright pink shorts riding his tan hairy thighs. When he reached them, he said to Alicia, "Don't hurt little Quenty. He is oh so fragile."

Quentin groaned.

Alicia smiled. "Hey, Eli."

Immediately dropping to his knees, Eli grabbed her

hand. His scarred tan face stared up at her as he said, "My sweet pop tart. Oh, how beautiful you look this morning."

Alicia blushed and pulled away.

To interrupt that mess, Quentin asked, "Where's your little companion?"

"In my shorts," Eli said.

"I meant Dickens."

"Yeah you did."

"I'm serious, Elijah."

Launching to his feet, Eli thrust a finger at Quentin's nose. "So am I. And Dickens is prepping the boat."

"Dickens is deaf, blind, and a mute."

"Don't forget partially retarded."

"You are crazy, man," said Quentin. "You're letting him prep the boat?"

"Ever doubt Dickens again and I'll rip your throat out!" Eli spun around and marched through the sand to the docks in a raging fit.

Quentin laughed. "Whoa, hit a sensitive spot I guess."

"What's the deal with you two anyway?"

"Me and Eli...." He lifted his duffle bag and headed to the boat. "It's a long story."

The dock rocked from side to side.

Eli sucked up the foggy sky as he stood with his arms outstretched. The beginning of his meditation was cut off by voices behind him.

"I'm telling you there is something wrong, sir."

"You said they left two days ago? That isn't too long."

"My daughter was supposed to be back with her boyfriend last night for dinner."

"Mr. Kane, right? What is your daughter's name?"

"Anna. She left on a sailboat. I think called the... Preacher? She's not answering her cell phone."

"Oh yes, The Preacher, bunch of kids left on that.

You said they were supposed to be back yesterday? Well, maybe wait till tomorrow. You know kids do the craziest things. I remember one time I was a kid, and I found a rock and named him Thelonious."

Mr. Kane groaned. "You are no help."

"Sorry," the other man responded and left Mr. Kane alone.

Eli couldn't help but spin around. "You say you got kids out there?"

Squinting at the shark hunter like he'd never heard a man speak before, Mr. Kane said, "Yeah. Why?"

"I'm heading out on a deadly voyage today. A voyage to slay the beast that lurks these waters."

"What?"

"I'll bring them kids back. You know how far out they went?"

"Well, my daughter said they were just SNUBA diving off the coast, so I'm assuming they are close but this damn fog."

Eli nodded, shutting his eyes. "Interesting."

"What is? And what beast is out there?"

"Don't worry." Eli patted Mr. Kane's arm. "I'll find your kids. I'll find your shark. I'll kill your shark."

"What? My shark? Who the hell are you?"

"I'm Elijah Augustus." He turned his back to Mr. Kane and flashed his head to the side. "Shark hunter."

RED

The remaining friends, except for Trisha, stood on the main deck of the sinking sailboat. Del couldn't believe she was dead. *I did what I could*, he told himself. *I know I did.*

Zeke was on his knees. "What are we going to do?"

"How long till we're in the water?" Vicki asked.

Willie, holding her hand, shrugged as he looked at the lowering bow. "I don't know. Half hour?"

"I don't believe this!" Zeke turned to Del. "And Trisha? She's really gone?"

"I thought she was okay. She seemed—"

"You only took two years of med school, dumb ass! You don't know shit!"

Del considered himself a calm dude who wouldn't snap unless someone tried hard enough. Zeke tried hard enough. Striking a hand around his neck, Del shoved him against the ladder leading to the upper deck and said, "You talk a big game, Zeke, but if you hadn't pushed Trisha in the water, she'd still be alive!" He tightened his grip. "Maybe Ray and Anna, too!"

Saliva flew out of Zeke's mouth as he yelled and choked.

Willie grabbed Del's large arm. "Enough. Let him go. We need to figure out how to get out of here."

An eerie creak echoed as the front of the ship inched

toward the water.

After letting go of Zeke, Del turned his back to his coughing friend and stared out at the ocean. He knew what needed to be done.

"Sailing is out of the question now," Vicki said then touched his lower back. "What are you thinking, Del?"

He swallowed, maybe even gulped. "We swim."

Zeke threw up his arms. "Are you out of your mind? You can't outswim a shark. Not to mention we still don't know where land is."

Del clenched his lips, hating himself for what he was about to say. "What if we throw Trisha's body overboard and use her as a distraction? If one of us can make it back to land, just one of us, then they can send help."

"One of us?" laughed Zeke. "Which one of us is dumb enough to get in the water?"

"We draw straws again like we did for Anna's body." Everyone stared at Del like he was the craziest man in the world. He added, "You three have any better ideas?"

Willie shook his fluffy hair. "Del! We don't know where land is or how far out we are now. I hate to say it, but Zeke is right. This idea is suicide."

"And staying on this boat isn't?" Del asked. "We are sinking right into that asshole's mouth!"

"Valid point also."

Del nodded. "I'll do it."

"What?"

"I'm in the best shape out of all of us. I can do it. Someone help me with Trisha's body."

Zeke stared at Willie and Vicki. "See? I'm not the psycho."

Throughout his life, Zeke had not seen many crazy things, except maybe a video of a penguin orgy. As he watched Del and Willie lower Trisha's pale, motionless body at the edge of the boat, he knew he'd see nothing crazier unless the shark decided to grab a mic and start some freestyle rap.

Willie stared up at Del. "Think about this, man. What direction are you betting on?"

Del dropped a pair of flippers, a mask and snorkel on the deck. He cracked his back and glanced around. "I say we drop her body here, and I hop off the other side. I heard a couple of seagulls earlier, I think in that direction. That means land is close, right?"

Willie shrugged.

Unbelievable, thought Zeke. He stared at Del and Willie one last time and then motioned for the upper deck to join Vicki.

He paused.

If that was going to be the last time he saw his friend, it had to be on good terms. "Del...."

"I'm doing this, man. I have to."

"I know," Zeke said. "Just, I'm sorry, bro. For all the jokes that offended you, for all the shit. I'm sorry."

Del looked at him as if the reality of what he was about to do had finally sunk in. He grabbed Zeke's hand, shook it, and the two of them hugged.

"The Triple P," Zeke whispered.

"Forever," Del said.

Trisha's face was turned away from Willie.

Her skin so pale and void of life, he couldn't believe another of them had died. Killed by a shark, no less.

Trisha still had a snorkel mask wrapped around her neck, and that made him laugh internally. He said to himself, "This is really happening."

Del grabbed him. Sweat dripped down the sides of his dark face, and his eyes were wide open. "We have to do this. Look at the ship."

The front of the boat was feet from descending under, while the back of it started to rise.

"We should squeeze blood out of her leg into the water first," Willie said.

"Why?"

"To attract the shark. Then we will know it's on this side of the boat, giving you a chance."

Del gulped.

"This idea sinking in yet?" Willie asked.

"Already has, but I have to do this." He looked at Trisha. "It's my fault she is dead. It's my fault I wasn't there for Ray or Anna. I can save the rest of us."

Willie's mouth hung open, but he voiced no words. He grabbed the back of Del's neck, locked eyes with him, and had they been lovers, they would've looked ready to share a kiss. He said to Del, "Thank you."

They let go.

Holding Trisha's dried-up calf, Willie unraveled the red shirt covering her wound. He moved the limb over the ledge of the ship and then squeezed his fingers against her skin.

A chunk of something plopped from her leg and splashed into the water, and a small stream of blood followed, and Willie wanted to cry.

As Del prepared himself to jump in the ocean, as Willie squeezed the bait into the water, as Zeke and Vicki hid on the upper deck, and as the large dorsal fin broke the surface and the caudal fin swerved its way to the ship, Trisha opened her eyes.

No one ever noticed.

FAIL

"It's coming!" screamed Willie. "Get ready, Del!"

Eyes widened, Trisha realized his hands were on her back. She knew he couldn't see her face as he started to shove. Why was he shoving? Why was he sending her into the ocean? Maybe she was still asleep and dreaming.

Through her pain and her confusion, she saw the dorsal fin of the shark.

Trisha's words were a throat-tearing scream as she fell into the water.

Right after hearing the scream, Del tossed his fins to the side and rushed across the deck to Willie. They watched Trisha splashing around in a panic.

"You told us she was dead," Willie said.

Del wondered how he could've been so wrong. She hadn't been breathing, had no pulse. He knew she was dead. *Knew it.*

It no longer mattered.

The shark darted right for the helpless Trisha, but it wouldn't get her or any more of Del's friends. He readied to redeem himself for all the mistakes he'd made throughout his life.

He dove for her.

"Go! Go!" Willie waved as he ran along the edge of the boat.

Reaching the rope ladder, Del had one arm wrapped around Trisha. He seemed focused yet terrified. Behind them, the shark disappeared below the surface, fins and all.

"It went under!" Willie screamed. Because the front of the boat was sinking, the part of the main deck where he stood was only a couple feet above the water.

"Grab her," Del said as he heaved her up.

Willie reached and—

In a blink of an eye, both Del and Trisha vanished.

Frozen in place, Willie stared at the white bubbly saltwater. Mist tickled his cheeks as if it were making fun of him. He couldn't believe he'd lost Del and Trisha in the same place where Ray was taken.

"Wh-what happened?" he asked himself and then screamed the question so maybe Zeke or Vicki would have an answer.

They didn't respond.

A wave rose, shooting across the deck and striking Willie's face.

Del made it onto the boat, but Willie couldn't go to him because he was locked in place. If anyone could've moved while seeing what he saw, he'd praise them forever.

Del screamed from within the mouth of the shark. Its teeth were sunk deep into his lower back. Its snout was just inches from Willie's legs.

Flailing, Del slapped Willie's knees as he tried to grab them and screamed, "Help me! *Help me.*"

The shark's jaws rose and slammed shut. Del cocked his head up, blood ejecting through his teeth.

A red wave covered Willie.

The great white bashed its head onto the main deck of the sailboat, thrashing. One of Del's wrists slapped

Willie across the face. The poor guy screamed like someone was peeling his skin off.

Engulfed in shock, Willie fell onto his shoulder, and for the briefest of moments, he locked eyes with the beast. He thought sharks were supposed to have lifeless eyes, eyes void of emotion, but in that shark's eyes, he saw something burning.

An anger he could not explain.

After a few swings, the shark slammed its head on the deck again. Willie heard the crunching of bones.

Somehow Delford was still alive, his veins thick in his face. He stretched a weak hand for Willie and said, "I tried…."

The shark flipped back into the water. The top half of Del's body ripped from its teeth and flung into the air. A rain of blood and intestines spiraled around in the gray sky as the remains of his corpse landed in the ocean.

Zeke needed a beer, or a shot of whiskey, or a joint, or a line of cocaine, or a hit of ecstasy, or any fucking thing to erase the last few minutes.

Standing next to Vicki, he watched red water wash onto the main deck, inches from his frozen friend.

"Willie!" Vicki screamed. "Get over here, Willie! Get away from the water!"

He stared at them like he no longer understood words.

Zeke had never seen such a lost look on his friend's face. He lowered his chin to his chest, knowing none of them were surviving that day. When Vicki grabbed his arm, he nearly cried.

"Go down there, Zeke. Help Willie."

Disbelief covered his face as he said, "Are you kidding me? Going to save someone equals a death sentence."

Despite his fleeting hope, Zeke still wanted to live and would do anything to make sure he saw land again.

Going down to the main deck would lessen his chance of survival, but Willie....

The shark returned, and Zeke turned away so he didn't have to see another one of them get eaten. Vicki slapped him. They locked eyes.

"It's going to kill him," she said. "Help your friend!"

His friend? Ray and Del were his friends, and they died, so he didn't want Willie to be his friend anymore because all of his friends get killed. His throat was so dry as he swallowed that in. "I...."

"Come on."

"Shut up, Vick. You have two hands, you go help him."

Together, they turned back to the mayhem below.

After coming to his senses, Willie realized he was too close to the water. He started to crawl up the wooden deck, toward the yells of Vicki. He'd do anything to be close to her voice again, and didn't even look back when the water rose behind him.

A large crack struck throughout the wet wooden floor.

Willie scrambled, reaching for the front mast, but it seemed to be moving farther away. He realized he was slipping back.

"No!" Vicki screamed. "Behind you!"

He caved in and looked. The great white's mouth was on the boat, snapping open and shut, trying to eat his chubby little legs.

Losing control of his limbs, he slid right to rows of teeth as long as his fingers. He waved his hands around trying to grab something or someone. Maybe Vicki would catch him, or maybe his mother would hold him and carry him away from the monster in the water.

Nothing was keeping him away from the shark.

Willie scrambled on his back, kicking gums and teeth.

One foot pressed against its snout and his other against the lower part of its mouth, he stared inside the beast, right into the pit of darkness that was its stomach. Stained in its teeth were pieces of human flesh. Dark flesh. Del's flesh.

When Willie noticed a girl's hand near its gums, he swore he saw her finger move.

Oh, screw that! He pushed off the snout, flipped onto his belly, and flailed his way up the deck.

Using every inch of his strength, he made one last lunge for the front mast.

He landed short of it, a shy kiss away.

The shark's mouth was wide open, a mechanical beast waiting to be fed again. Or maybe it just wanted to kill.

Willie slid toward his casket right as Zeke grabbed his wrist.

"Kick to me!" his friend commanded. He had his other arm wrapped around the mast.

He did kick, all the way back to Zeke, and the two of them hugged the mast together, their trembling faces close.

"Thank you," Willie said. "Thank you, Zeke."

The shark shut its mouth and sank back into a sea of blood.

While the chaos ensued outside, the interior of the sailboat was silent, save for a muffled vibrating noise. Anna had brought a pink duffle bag aboard the ship. In the side pocket of the bag, buried beneath some articles of clothing, was her mobile phone and an incoming call from her father.

HELL

The twenty-eight-foot fiberglass fishing boat navigated the Pacific Ocean through the foggy sky. At the front of the white boat, Quentin Samuels and Alicia Alvarez stood together, salty mist splashing their faces. Several feet behind them was the center console where Elijah Augustus manned the wheel. He drank a 40 oz of beer and hummed a Katy Perry song. Behind Eli, Dickens prepared buckets of chum to be dumped overboard.

Quentin squinted at Alicia, his fro bouncing in the wind. "I doubt he even knows where we're going."

"I'll talk to him."

"Wait, maybe I should. He can be… intoxicating."

Alicia laughed. "Relax, I can handle him."

"Okay. But we still need to have *our* talk."

"We will, babe. Don't you worry that pretty face of yours."

Smiling, Quentin playfully punched Alicia's life jacket and said, "Wouldn't dream of it." His body warmed as he watched her walk away, and he thought, *Our mission out at sea is what will bring us back together. I know it. We will no longer be mad or resentful. We will be one. We will be love.*

Bringing the 40 oz to his mouth to finish it off, Elijah stared at Alicia as she approached him. He wanted to do beautiful things to her, very beautiful things.

When he dropped the glass bottle to the floor, Alicia skipped over it and said, "Whoa. Careful."

Eli lowered his Ray-Ban sunglasses down his large nose. "Worst case scenario? The glass cuts my flesh, and I give my blood to the shark, just before I impale its eyes with my thumbs."

"Uh, so, how are you going to find it?"

"It finds me."

"Listen." Alicia scratched her neck. "We have a lot riding on this. We can't just go out for a joy sail."

Eli let go of the wheel, marched right to her, and threw his sunglasses into the ocean. His eyes bulged from their sockets. "You think I joy sail? You think I don't take this seriously?" He grabbed Alicia's hand and made her finger slide down the large scar engraved from his forehead to his chin. "You ever have a shark eat your face?"

"Eli… I—"

"Save it." He went to push his sunglasses up his nose but realized he threw them in the ocean. "Damn, not again."

Alicia followed him back under the center console and grabbed his shoulder. "Listen. I know you want this as bad as I do. Just make sure we find it."

"Will do, sugar cube."

From the bow of the boat, Quentin watched them. Eli could see the jealousy in his eyes and asked Alicia, "How long were you and Quenty playing chutes and ladders for?"

"A few years, why?"

"So you like vagina?"

"What? Quentin is a man."

"Yeah and I once went to a John Mayer concert."

Alicia laughed at that one. "You're kind of funny actually. Stupid but funny."

"When you've been close to death like me, you tend

to see the world differently."

"How so?" asked Quentin, stepping up to the side of the console.

Eli shot a clump of spit by his foot. "I'd rather be eaten by a shark than tell you."

"Fine. Just explain to us what we're doing, Eli."

"Finding the shark."

"And when we find it," Alicia said, "what's the plan?"

One hand on the wheel, Eli stared straight ahead at the face of the cruelly gorgeous sea. "There is only one way to kill this beast."

"How?"

"Dickens, bring me the crate!"

The short, pudgy man was still playing with the chum behind Eli. Blood and meat had spilled out onto the white fiberglass of the boat.

"I thought he was deaf?" Quentin asked.

"You know I'd hit you if you weren't a woman," Eli responded.

"Enough! Why do you still hate me, man?"

Eli let go of the wheel, grabbed Quentin's white T-shirt, and shoved him until his back cracked over the metal railing of the boat.

"Eli!" the weak man pleaded, his head nearly touching the water. "Let me up!"

"Feel it coming, don't you? Sensing its teeth wanting to shred you apart?"

"Let go of him!" Alicia demanded.

When Eli felt someone touch his shoulder, he instantly cocked his elbow back.

On the ground, Alicia grabbed her bleeding face. He fell next to her and said, "My spicy tuna, I did not mean to! You can't sneak up on me like that."

She shoved away from him, and while holding her face, stumbled to the cushioned V-berth at the front of the boat.

Quentin pushed Eli, but the man didn't budge. "You asshole."

"Assholes take long clean shits, my friend, and I don't take long clean shits."

"What?"

Just then, Dickens dragged a wooden crate to the middle of the boat, right in front of the center console. Eli knelt over the crate and uncovered it.

"What's in there?" Alicia asked as she wiped the little bit of blood dripping from her nose.

"In here is how we kill the beast."

"How is that?"

"There is only one way we can kill it." Eli stood, and in his hand was a stick of dynamite. "Explode it back to hell."

DEEP

Sitting on the white cushioned bench of the fiberglass fishing boat, Quentin Samuels stared at the clearing fog. Visibility was still hindered, as was his patience.

He knew finding the shark would take some time, but he also knew that idiot Eli didn't have a plan, and they'd been circling around the coast for far too long.

However, what bothered him most was watching Alicia fall for Eli's mannish charms by the center console of the boat. She leaned close to him, giggling at his stupidity.

Quentin had to look away. He hated how angry he got when Alicia talked to another man but couldn't help himself even though he knew better. It wasn't at all healthy, at least that was what his therapist had said. Although to be fair, he'd stop seeing his therapist because she didn't know what she was talking about.

Sometimes it felt like Quentin was surrounded by idiots, like he was the only sane person left in a decompensating world.

The fishing boat slowed down.

Now what? he wondered as he faced the captain. His eyes widened, and he lifted to his feet, thinking, *No, no not her.*

At the center console, Eli stood inches from Alicia's face,

looking into her auburn eyes and grazing the side of her tan cheek with his rough fingers. "You are a sacchariferous kumquat."

Alicia blushed. "Oh, quit it, Eli."

Wrapping an arm around the small of her back, he pulled her close. His upper lip lifted. "Don't you feel that stinging heat of passion burning between our loins?"

Even though she tried to resist, she couldn't help but lock onto his eyes. She brushed a hand up through his large mane of brown hair, which smelled like Moroccan oil and was surprisingly soft. But it was the manliness of his face that charmed her. *Such a man*, she thought, *such a damn man.*

More importantly, though, Alicia just wanted to control Eli, and she thought giving him a kiss would give her the upper hand. She parted her lips slightly, inviting him to make a move.

"What the hell are you two doing?" Jaw-dropped, Quentin stared at them.

Eli's face snapped to the side. "Relax, Quenty. I'm about to make you a godfather."

Alicia shoved off the shark hunter. "We were just talking."

"Yeah, let's call it that." Eli chuckled to himself and wiped his mouth.

Quentin pointed at him. "I would expect this from you! But you, Alicia? I thought we had something and all you've been doing is flirting with this guy."

Alicia laughed. "Relax, okay? This is strictly business."

"The business of furious mating," Eli said.

Rubbing her temple, Alicia shut her eyes. "We need to find the shark. We must forget everything else. The shark is too important." She looked up at Eli, who still had a smirk crossing the side of his face. "Okay?"

"Of course, my delectable potato pancake."

Quentin groaned as he pinched the top of his nose. "Shut. Up."

"Listen." Alicia stepped toward him. "How about we talk in a bit, okay? I know I owe you a talk, but right now we need to relax. We need to find the—"

"The shark?" Quentin's face flushed to a burning red. He threw his hands up and stepped to the front of the fishing boat. "Where are we gonna find the damn shark? You two act like sharks are just out here to eat us. You know nothing about them and are so far off it's getting to be ridiculous. I mean, it's astonishing how out of your minds the two of you are. You think they desire human flesh. Ha! It's crazy. It's not real. It's stupid. Laughable!" He pointed at Eli. "For the last damn time, sharks *don't* hunt us."

The ocean exploded. A gray and white mouth snatched Quentin between its teeth, taking him across the boat and into the water.

Alicia watched in shock as the back of the shark dove under.

Quentin was gone.

At her side, Eli's hands tightened into fists. "Dickens," he growled. "Prepare the dynamite."

SIGHT

Sunshine fought the foggy sky.

On the upper deck overlooking the rest of the sinking boat, Zeke had half a mind to go grab the wheel in the cockpit and pretend he was a captain going down with his ship. That thought saddened him. His shoulders dropped, and he was ready to cry as he tucked his head toward his lap.

A seagull, he swore he heard one. He hated seagulls. Squawking, and flapping, and pooping everywhere, and

———

Wait, he thought. *If there are seagulls, then land must be close.*

At least he hoped that true.

Zeke's head shot up from his lap. The seagull flew through breaking fog, and in front of it was indeed land. His throat was so dry as he said, "Guys. Look."

Willie and Vicki weakly watched as Zeke pointed at salvation.

Vicki scratched her sunburnt tan skin. "How far out are we?"

"About a mile?" Willie stood and looked at Zeke for reassurance.

"I have no fucking clue."

Vicki stepped to the ladder leading to the main deck. The ocean was close to reaching the mast at the center of the boat.

"Where are you going?" Willie asked her, his fluffy hair blowing around like it was dancing.

"I saw some knives in the kitchen. I think we could use some weapons."

He raised his eyebrows, turned to Zeke, and said, "Yep, I'm in love." He then rushed to Vicki's side and followed her down the ladder. Once on the main deck, he shouted at Zeke, "Yell if you see the shark, yeah?"

"Just make it quick. The water is rising fast."

Willie stared at him like it could be the last time, then entered the interior of the sailboat.

After collapsing into the captain's swivel chair, Zeke stared at land and was surprised Del was going to jump in the right direction.

An ill feeling engulfed him as he thought about Del and Ray. The three of them had been a three-prong power plug, the Triple P, and now it was only him.

"A single P," he whispered alone.

Scratching his head, Zeke was surprised his blond fohawk was still gelled up. *Well, I gotta look good for my date with the shark.* But joking around only made him want to cry, so he figured he'd do something to take his mind off his shitty situation.

He hummed that song from *Jaws* before the shark attacked the boat at the end of the movie. He couldn't remember the name of it, and hardly knew any of the words.

His humming died, and he stared at the rising water, which surpassed the middle mast by a few inches. The sea was about eight feet away from flooding the cabin of the sailboat.

Zeke called down to his friends, "Guys, hurry up!"

No response.

Knowing he needed to be a better lookout, he searched for the wretched beast hunting them down.

Why did it so badly want to kill them? Why them? He never did anything to that shark. He would even be its friend.

All of my friends die. Zeke fell back in his chair. If anyone had asked him if he ever expected to be hunted by a shark, he would've slapped that person silly.

Now he'd hug them because seeing anyone else meant he was finally saved.

When he saw the tall, dark dorsal fin again, he knew his chances of survival were next to none.

Scavenging the kitchen, Vicki knocked over a couple pots. She swung open a wooden drawer, pulled out two large steak knives, then turned around and tossed one to Willie, who stood near Anna's pink duffle bag.

Although the blade nearly slashed his wrist, he found her desire to arm themselves incredibly badass and sexy. But he didn't want to get cut and told her to be careful.

"Sorry. I'm out of it." Vicki pressed against the sink. "I've been so out of it since Anna, and then Del, and I froze and couldn't help you, and I just want to go home."

Willie stepped over the duffle bag and reached for her hand. "It's okay, just… wait. What is that?"

"Huh?"

"Listen." His eyes wandered to the bag. "It's vibrating." He rushed to his knees, unzipped the bag, and yanked out Anna's belongings until he pulled out the vibrating phone.

The incoming call from Anna's father ended. She had six missed calls from him.

"It was here all this time. Holy shit." Vicki dropped to her knees by Willie, and a bright smile crossed her face. "I love you, Anna, I really do." She took the phone from him and called Anna's father back.

"Mr. Kane? This is Vicki. We are still on the boat."

She lowered her head. "Mr. Kane, please listen. It's about Anna. We… we were attacked, and her and Ray…."

Willie was about to grab the phone to help her, when Zeke started yelling at them to get back to the upper deck.

"*Shark*," Zeke shouted several times.

As Vicki spoke with Anna's father, Willie climbed into the square entryway of the cabin and searched the sinking deck.

The shark circled the boat.

Willie mumbled to himself, "Not again." He spun around and reached for Vicki, and although he should panic because of their situation, he fixated on the glow in Vicki's eyes when she spoke. Even her hints of sadness stirred his nerve endings.

With his back to the water, Willie said, "Let's get going, Vicki."

She nodded at him, the phone to her ear. "Okay bye, Mr. Kane. Th-thank you." She hung up and slipped it into the pocket of Anna's white jacket and then stared up at Willie. Her lips flashed white teeth, a smile indicating not all hope was lost. "They're coming for us, Willie. We're saved."

AMENDS

Sitting on the benches of the upper deck, Zeke, Willie, and Vicki watched the fin of the shark as it swam around the sinking boat.

"It's waiting till we're in the water." Willie tightened his arm around Vicki. "I'm guessing we have no more than fifteen minutes."

"Great," Zeke said. "I could use a dip in the ocean."

Somehow Vicki laughed at that. She asked, "Should we swim for it?"

Willie rubbed her hand, which Zeke assumed was an attempt at comforting her. He said, "We won't have a choice soon."

"Great."

All things considered, Zeke thought, *they actually look pretty cute holding each other.* He stood and stared at the completely submerged front of the boat, a sight that made his muscles tense. He went to the back of the deck, grabbed the railing to maintain his balance, and looked down at the water. The back of the boat was rising out of the ocean, which was also a terrifying sight.

Then, the dark gray silhouette of the shark glided below him, and he wanted to shit himself.

"It just passed underneath," he said. "What if we leap on it with knives and slice it up?"

Willie tilted his head. "Just fight the asshole to

death?"

"Three on one. We could do it."

"No," Willie said. "But I wish this were a movie, too."

Zeke stared at the knives in both Willie and Vicki's hands. "So what do you plan on doing with those things?"

"When we go under, aim for its eyes and gills."

Zeke didn't know why but hearing that made him want to give them hugs. He figured he owed them an apology before they went into the water. "Listen, guys. I just want to say, um, sorry I've been an asshole."

"It's fine, buddy."

"We have bigger things to worry about," Vicki added.

Thinking it'd be nice to solidify amends with a couple of handshakes, Zeke stepped to his friends.

The sailboat was struck.

Thrown to the side, Zeke grabbed the railing, managing to stay on the deck yelling, "Motherfucking shark!"

Willie crawled for Zeke, reaching for him. "Get back in the middle with us."

As he helped his friend, Vicki stood and looked over the side of the boat for the shark. She wanted to be done hiding, done whining, and done being the pretty girl no one took seriously. Her fingers tightened around her knife, ready to stab the asshole that killed her friends.

For Anna and Ray. Del. Even Trisha. I'll kill you for them.

She heard Willie yell, "Come on, man!"

Zeke seemed frozen with fear as he held dearly to the railing at the back of the boat.

I'll get him down. She stepped toward the boys, legs wobbling for balance.

For some reason, her feet no longer touched the deck, and she was falling.

The shark had hit the ship again, she realized, and

she was in the ocean.

Willie and Zeke looked at each other with relief; however, a scream echoed behind them, followed by a splash.

They spun around. Vicki was gone.

"VICKI!" Willie rushed to the side of the boat, leaned over the railing, and stared at white bubbles.

Seconds later, she splashed to the surface. "Help! Please help!"

"Hang on!" Willie climbed onto the bench. "I'm coming."

Zeke shot a hand for his friend. "What are you doing, man? Don't do it. You're dead if you do. Just like Ray, just like Del. Don't go in there for her."

Ignoring his friend's wise words, Willie clutched the steak knife firmly and with confidence he said, "To quote the great Sir Anthony Hopkins, *Today, I'm gonna kill the muthafucka.*"

"Don't!"

Willie leaped over the side of the sailboat.

THREE

All his focus was on her. Whatever it took, Willie would get Vicki out of the water.

Their strokes were sloppy and frantic as they swam for the sinking sailboat, which was maybe fifteen feet away. From the upper deck, Zeke yelled, "Go! Swim!"

Willie wanted to ask him where the shark was, but he just kept his eyes on Vicki, who swam in front of him.

Ten feet away.

He knew he'd do anything to make sure she got out of the water first. As he raced behind her, he kept his hand wrapped around his large knife. He was ready to stab, *no*, itching to stab the freak of nature that wanted their blood.

Five feet away.

"I don't see it," Zeke called down. "Just keep swimming. Come on!"

When Vicki reached the sailboat, Willie pushed her legs up, hoping she'd quickly get to safety. He glanced up at Zeke. "See it?"

"I don't! Not yet. I don't see it!"

Willie could tell his friend was panicking, probably worse than himself, but he also knew those who panicked were those who died.

With Vicki out of the water, Willie reached for the ladder leading to the upper deck. His knees rested on the submerged main deck, water splashing at his waist.

Then he heard the words rip from Zeke's mouth: "*Behind you.*"

But he didn't look back because those who hesitated were those who died.

On his feet, Willie grabbed the ladder and started to climb. Vicki was trembling in the entryway to the cabin.

He smiled at her.

Standing by the entrance to the cabin, Vicki screamed as she watched the shark turn on its side, revealing its white belly. Its pectoral fin sliced the surface, and its mouth opened wide around Willie's legs.

In one splash, Willie was yanked from Vicki's sight, leaving the top of the ocean empty. She shivered as she lowered to her knees. A small wave hit her face but she didn't care. Willie had been right next to her. *Right next to her.*

He was gone, but she said his name and said it again, hoping he would answer.

An eye full of anger looked right at him as he was dragged underwater.

Willie bashed his fist against the sandpapery skin of the shark. He knew he was in its mouth, but it took him a minute to realize it had him by his calves.

Thinking it was going to take him down until he drowned, Willie was surprised to breathe again. He used all of his power and swung forward. He grabbed the top of the shark, readied the knife near its eye, and—

The shark bit harder on his legs, and he let out a miserable cry of pain. He went underwater again, then broke the surface, then under, then broke it again.

Had he lost his knife? He wasn't sure. Everything happened so quickly, he couldn't even tell if he was underwater or not. *The knife? Where is the knife?!*

Then he saw Anna, remembering the look in her eyes as he held her over the side of the boat, right before he lost her. She was dead. They all were. All of them killed by the wretched beast.

But Willie still had his knife.

"Get gutted, you bitch!" He stabbed at the shark's eye.

The beast jerked its head, causing him to miss and stab the knife into gray skin. He quickly yanked it out and swung again.

The shark squeezed harder.

There was a loud crunch, a haunting crunch; then he was free from its mouth.

Surrounded in blood, Willie splashed frantically until he found his bearings. The shark, not far in front of him, chomped up and down on someone's calves and feet as if it were mocking him. Then it vanished below.

Those weren't mine, he thought. *How could those be mine?*

He felt nothing past his knees but still wasn't ready to give up.

Bleeding, woozy, and legless, Willie swam for the boat.

He saw Vicki in the entryway of the cabin and was about to yell her name but saltwater poured into his mouth. Choking, he swam, and he didn't stop swimming until he reached the submerged deck of the boat.

"Help," he moaned to Vicki.

She said nothing, but the look in her eyes made him turn around.

A rush of water hit his face. Something sharp stabbed his back. His chest was smashed, stealing what breath he had left.

The sky mixed with the ocean and the cries of his friends drowned to nothing, but Willie still had his knife. He screamed Vicki's name and thrust his blade into the beast.

Vicki shut her eyes. She had to. *It wasn't him. Not him.*
He'd been nice to her, so nice, even saved her. *The nice
guys don't get killed*, she told herself. *They don't.*

Wishes were for idiots.

Still refusing to look at the water, Vicki focused on
her racing heart. It was beating so quickly she thought it
would collapse at any moment from exhaustion. When
it finally slowed down, it sank like the sailboat because it
knew the reality of the world she lived in. *But maybe,* she
thought, *maybe if I just stay here it will all be over. None of it
will be true and it will all be over.*

A wave hit her neck. She opened her eyes and a
painful lump in her throat told her hope was something
best left for those on land.

Willie's decapitated head bobbed up and down, three
feet away from her toes.

STUCK

On his hands and knees, spit hanging from his lips, Zeke stared at the red ocean.

Willie's head was gone, and Zeke didn't know if it sank, floated away, or was eaten by that dickhole of a fish. He supposed it didn't matter because either way his friend was dead. *Dead because of her.*

Since Willie had died saving Vicki, Zeke mumbled her name to see if she was still down there. No answer. He yelled her name. Nothing.

Crawling to the edge of the upper deck looking over the rest of the sunken ship, Zeke kept yelling for her. She was in the entryway of the cabin, pale and still.

"Look at me," he said.

She didn't.

"Will you look at me, Vicki? My friend just died saving your slutty ass!"

Her eyes were as dead as all the others. "He's gone."

"I know." Zeke sighed. "Look, sorry I called your ass slutty, but just grab my hand, Victoria."

"Why?"

"Why? WHY? The shark will get you, man. *Now grab my damn hand.*"

Her lips were chapped and shaking as she said, "Okay."

"Good, that's good."

Zeke was so close to touching her when a sharp wave blasted across them.

The shark lunged for Vicki. She vanished from Zeke's sight, along with the tips of his fingers.

Falling on his back, he raised his hand over his face. Blood poured out his middle and ring fingers. *It got me*, he thought, *holy shit it got me.*

And he yelled, "Why are you so pissed off, shark?"

Vicki dropped into the cabin.

On her back, she stared up at the entryway. The shark's mouth frantically twisted and snapped open and shut, trying to break in to devour her. Its thrashing weight caused the sailboat to sink quicker.

She stayed on the floor, releasing slow and even breaths. *I should be panicking*, she thought. *I should be crying and screaming and running for my life.*

Instead, Vicki crawled to the back of the cabin and on to the V-berth. She stared at the shark and the ocean, knowing she was trapped.

I'm going to die here. To think otherwise is stupid.

The shark eventually disappeared but the invading ocean reached the V-berth. Coldness touched her toes. She lifted her legs and tucked them against her breasts.

Lips hanging open and shivering in place, Vicki scooted to the deepest corner of the cabin, hoping the water would leave her alone.

In the hopeless distance, Zeke shouted, and she thought it sweet of him to still be worried about her, but she wasn't leaving that berth. Why would she? As much as she feared drowning, it still sounded better than the shark's teeth ripping her in half like Anna and Del, and Willie, Ray… and Trisha.

Vicki never hated that girl. Sure, she got annoyed with her, but she never *hated* her. *Now Trisha is dead. They're all dead, and I did nothing.*

All my life I've done nothing.

Vicki wanted to break into tears, but soon her face would be wet enough.

Until then, her eyes stayed dry.

He could hear the shark splashing around below him.

Rolling back and forth, grabbing the tips of his bleeding fingers, Zeke gritted his teeth. He yelled, he cried, he pleaded. He wished he knew a prayer or anything to save him from his imminent death.

As his lips trembled, Zeke realized they weren't trembling for the pain in his hand or the uncertainty of his fate, but only for his friends. Ray and Del, he'd never been that nice to them, he supposed, but he did love them, his two other prongs. He hoped they had known all of that before they died. And Willie, *fucking Willie.*

His lips trembled again, for his family. They'd never know what exactly happened there and probably wouldn't even believe the story if he got the chance to tell them. They'd just know he was gone. Dead.

His lips trembled again. That time for his ex-girlfriend. He'd lost her over one of the dumbest things possible, for being a chronic masturbator.

Who loses someone over such a thing? Oh yeah, this asshole.

All Zeke wanted was one more chance to see his loved ones again, to see his ex and explain his chronic masturbating problem.

The splashing stopped, leaving his world in silence.

Done wishing, hoping and regretting, Zeke pulled his T-shirt off and tied it around his hand. Blood quickly stained the fabric.

On his feet, he looked down at the main deck. The sea was flooding the interior of the boat, and once more, he yelled for Vicki.

Nothing.

Pacing in circles, Zeke yelled her name a few more times, and when she didn't respond, he decided she was a lost cause. He stared at the rising water, figuring he had maybe ten minutes before he'd have to swim, or in the more likely scenario, become a shark meal.

Either way I'm screwed.

However, when he noticed Vicki's steak knife by the captain's chair, he had an opportunity to go down fighting.

He had one last shot at a new life, his final battle against a man-eating beast.

GOODBYE

Alicia Alvarez stumbled forward on the white fiberglass fishing boat. Her legs throbbed before giving out.

Collapsed on the floor of the boat, her hands in Quentin's blood, she couldn't believe what she'd just seen. It took him, her mind kept saying, *the shark took him*.

She crawled to the edge of the boat and peeked over the railing to see his remains bobbing in the water. Disgusted, she flipped around and whispered Eli's name.

The shark hunter didn't hear her. His mane of brown hair growled with the wind as he stood cocked straight, staring into the ocean.

"Eli!" She rushed her palms over her eyes. "I got him killed."

When she lowered her hands, Eli was crouching in front of her. "Listen to me, Alicia." She was surprised he said *Alicia* and not some stupid nickname. "Quenty died with purpose, for the greater cause."

"The greater cause? Quentin is dead because I wanted to be rich. I even lied about the amount of money he—"

"We can still get the shark."

Alicia cracked her jaw. "Why did you hate Quentin?"

He glanced away.

"Tell me, Elijah. Tell me now."

"Back in the day. Back when this world had no Justin Bieber. Back when—"

"*Eli*. Be straight with me. For once, please be straight with me."

"Quentin." Eli hung his head and slid his finger down the scar crossing his face from his forehead to his chin. "Quentin had helped me on a quest, and was there when the shark bit my face. He even had a chance to kill it. But, well, Quenty wouldn't kill a shark. Couldn't. Killing didn't flow in his blood. Some say Quenty had too much sand in his loins, clouding his judgment, but truth is I'll never know."

Alicia slapped him. "You're still making jokes? Quentin is dead!"

Silence crossed the shark hunter's face. He glanced at the floor before saying in the sincerest of tones, "If I stop making jokes, then the shark wins."

She slapped him again. "Your shark killed Quentin."

"No." Eli stood, yanking Alicia to her feet. "Our shark."

She tried to push out of the man's grip but wasn't strong enough.

Suddenly his arms went limp, falling at his sides as he whispered, "Alicia."

The private investigator looked up at him. "What is it?"

"Turn around."

Wiping her face, she followed Eli's command, and when she saw the sinking sailboat, she said, "My God, Eli. My God."

"Not God." Eli lifted one foot onto the edge of the boat, resting his arms on his thigh like the captain he was. "Not God at all who did this."

RESCUE

Elijah Augustus throttled the fishing boat through the ocean, racing for the sinking sailboat. A young man waved his arms over his head, jumping up and down.

The fins of the beast circled him, hunting.

Eli hit the foghorn. He hit it again, hit it one more time. The shark descended beneath the surface.

"That a girl," the hunter said. "Come for Daddy." He turned around and slapped Dickens's back, who was hunched over the box of dynamite.

Alicia was close by, wiping the drying tears that had fallen for Quentin. She said, "Eli, you actually found them."

"Yes. I also found your shark."

"The one that ate Quentin?"

"It was smaller." Eli clenched the wheel. "Not your shark."

"What are you saying? There're two of them?"

"There are many sharks in this ocean."

"No shit." Some strength returned in her voice. "I'm talking about the man-eaters."

"So am I."

A large smile crossed Zeke's face as he stared at the fishing vessel speeding toward him. He spun around, dropped to the wood of the upper deck, crawled to the edge and looked at the submerged main deck. "Vicki! Help is here!"

No response.

"Vicki, come on! Get up here!" He was by the edge for almost a minute before he realized his head was too close to the water. He backed away, screaming, "Whatever! You want to die? Then die!"

Beneath Zeke, Vicki rocked back and forth in a ball on the V-berth.

The ocean water reached the bottom of the cushion, nearly splashing her bare feet. She stared at the reflection of her dry eyes in the ocean, hoping Zeke's cries would carry her to the upper deck of the boat.

Something wouldn't let her move, telling her she was safer in the cabin than outside of it. She knew it irrational, but while being squeezed into a little ball by pain and fear, there was no going anywhere.

Snap out of it, she told herself. *Snap out of it and go home.*

The berth tightened around her, and it wouldn't be long until the water did the same.

The all-white sailboat tilted to the side, descending beneath the ocean.

Alicia, at the front of Eli's boat, yelled, "We have to hurry!"

"Patience, my succulent triceratops. Just tighten your life jacket and be patient."

Alicia smiled. "Don't you mean death jacket?"

Eli focused on the young man atop the sailboat and wondered how many of his friends were dead. Not that it mattered, for as long as there was human flesh in its ocean, the beast would attack again.

Excitement filled Eli's knees as he thought—

Eli sniffed, sniffed twice. A shiver crawled down his spine, and he crept his head around, letting go of the wheel. "Dickens!"

In Eli's deaf, blind, mute, and partially retarded companion's hand was a stick of dynamite. The fuse was lit.

Eli fell to his knees and screamed, "You've murdered us all, Dickens!"

Zeke held onto the railing to help him balance on the tilting upper deck.

He watched the white fishing boat speed right for him and smiled because he was finally saved.

The boat vanished before his eyes, exploding into an orange fireball. Flaming pieces rained across the ocean.

On his legs, still holding the white railing above his head, Zeke couldn't help but laugh. *It exploded. Ha! It exploded.*

Water touched his feet, but he didn't care. He was done. He even laughed a few more times.

GONE

Alicia Alvarez's mouth shot open for air, and her hands splashed around pieces of flaming fiberglass. She wasn't sure what had happened, had just been sitting there when Eli told her to jump, and before she could act, she was thrown from the fishing boat by the explosion.

Touching her face with a shaking hand, Alicia felt burnt flesh. She cried in pain. Then she fully realized she was in the water and had no time to worry about the skin of her pretty face.

She spun around yelling, "Eli!"

He never responded. *Screw him*, she thought. She needed to save her own ass, so she swam for the sinking sailboat.

Vicki had moved from the V-berth, sitting on the tallest thing she could fit herself on, a counter in the galley.

The water filled a quarter of the cabin.

Staring at the light reflecting off the rising surface, Vicki knew her time to drown was seconds away. But at least she'd be spared death by shark.

Vanishing light, sweet vanishing light.

She wasn't sure why but she pulled Anna's phone from her pocket. It was soaked, broken, but maybe a call would come in saying she was saved. A voice was what she wanted, a voice to tell her everything would be okay. She even heard Anna's voice. It was cheerful and excited to go out at sea with her friends and spend the day SNUBA diving, swimming with—

SNUBA.

Vicki looked right at the white and blue SNUBA raft.

Zeke was still holding the white railing when the woman reached him. Half her face was melted mush. Her burnt hands slapped the boat, trying to get a solid grip. She was a few feet below him and screamed for help.

Drool fell off his smile. "We're dead," he said to her. "We are all dead."

"Help me. Please help me. Get me out and you're saved!"

Although he said something, he had no idea what it was.

"Help me! Help! Plea-"

The burnt woman's neck and head stiffened. Then she was gone, beneath the surface like all of the others.

Gulping, Zeke let go of the railing. Water touched his ass, but he really didn't care.

It's my time to swim with the mother of all fishes.

He decided to stand. Why not? He was dead either way, but at least he still had the knife.

I'll die fighting. Just like you, Willie. Just like you.

The water was up to his ankles as he searched for the shark.

"Come at me," he whispered, lifting the knife in the air. "You want me? Come get me!" His bare chest pumped in and out. "Come on! Where are you?" The water crept up his thighs to his waist. "Come on!" He kept yelling as he sank, waving the knife in every direction. "Come on!" Tears fell down his face. His lips trembled, and his head dropped. "Come, come on…."

Just then, out of the corner of his eye, as the water rose up to his stomach, causing his feet to release from the top of the sailboat, Zeke saw the dorsal fin approach him.

In the shark's mouth, the burnt woman flailed her arms around as she was eaten.

Zeke gripped the knife tighter in his trembling hand. His legs kicked him above the surface, the sailboat several feet beneath him.

Still chomping on the woman, the shark didn't seem to notice Zeke. However, he knew it would quickly find him.

His end had arrived.

Water filled the cabin without compassion.

Vicki had managed to pull herself together and shove the SNUBA raft out of the interior of the sailboat. She'd lost her grip on it, though, and it shot to the light without her.

There was still some breathing room in the cabin, just enough for her mouth to break wide against the ceiling. The water was at her neck. She sucked in all the oxygen her lungs could carry. Full of air, she shoved her face underwater and looked for the black bag containing the mask, flippers, and snorkels. Too dark to search for it and running out of time, she decided the SNUBA gear was a lost cause. But before she left it behind, she remembered seeing it underneath the tiny table hours earlier.

The saltwater burned her eyes as she swam down. Her feet pushed off the ceiling. She was pleasantly surprised the bag was still there, but when she yanked it, it didn't swim away with her. It was caught on something. *Of course it's caught on something.* She frantically tugged a few more times, but too much panic filled her limbs, and she let go.

Her head smacked the ceiling. Her lips broke open for the last bit of air.

She didn't want to go back under, never wanted to go under again, but she told herself to do it for Anna. *Everyone will know you died a hero, my love.*

Rubber and plastic hit her face right when she went under. She grabbed a mask and realized the bag had ripped open. *Finally, some luck.* She pressed her hands up, trying to touch the ceiling before hitting her head again.

Air never tasted so good, but it wouldn't last.

After somehow managing to get the mask over her head without water filling it, Vicki lowered and swam to the cabin entrance of the sailboat.

Slight streams of sunlight twinkled in the sea.

NEVER

A cluster of bubbles rose next to Zeke. *Another shark*! he thought as he swam around frantically. *A different shark is going to eat me.*

Like a prayer answered from below, the white and blue SNUBA raft blasted out of the water. He raced for it. Balancing on his knees, he bobbed up and down on the raft, surprised it supported his weight.

The burnt woman's blood was close to him, but there was no sign of her or the shark. Tan chunks of meat floated next to torched pieces of the fishing boat that had tried rescuing him. *Maybe her leftovers.* He didn't really care, but he did wonder why it exploded, and how many people were killed.

Bubbles behind him.

Zeke spun around, almost toppling into the water, waving his knife like a frantic fool. Luckily, it was no shark. Vicki. Having never expected to see her again, he couldn't stop himself from smiling. "Here. Over here!"

When she reached the raft, he tried lifting her onto it but knew it'd tip over. Only one of them could stay on top. He let go of her and looked at the land, guessing it half a mile away from them. He didn't want to trick himself into believing home was close.

Home would die like the others.

"Where is it?" Vicki asked as she lifted the snorkel

mask onto her head.

"Not sure. But we aren't waiting to find out." He lowered into the water.

"What are you doing?"

"You get on it."

She squinted in disbelief. "What?"

"Get on there, Vick."

She grabbed his face and kissed his cheek, then climbed onto the raft.

Zeke wasn't sure why he was doing it. Maybe he owed her something. Maybe he owed them all something.

Everyone died being selfless. Why shouldn't I?

Vicki handed him her mask, and he fixed it over his face. He then examined the tubes hanging off the raft. "Kind of wish we went diving the other day, so I knew what to do."

Vicki handed him a regulator. "Stick it in your mouth and breathe."

Zeke almost cracked a joke but gave her a smile instead.

Before he went under, Vicki grabbed his wrist and said, "Thank you."

"In case we don't make it, I—"

"Just get us into a dry towel."

They headed home.

Zeke kept one hand on the rear white underbelly of the raft as he kicked and paddled, breathing through the regulator connected to a yellow hose. He still had his other hand around the steak knife.

All he could hear was the sound of his heart beating against his chest as he gazed at the empty ocean, searching for the predator hunting them. He knew it lurked in the dark reaches, stalking him.

Or maybe it didn't know where they were?

No, he thought, *that's a stupid thing to think*. The shark knew exactly where they were and where they'd been. It knew everything, a freak of nature no one would ever likely cross paths with again.

Looking around, Zeke knew the shark could come out of the dark at any time and get him without warning. But he couldn't think about that. All he could do was swim forward, keep moving forward, and never look back.

The raft pushed faster. Vicki hoped Zeke didn't see something and was okay.

While lying flat on the raft, she paddled on each side, and all she did was stare straight for land. It wasn't too far away. She even saw a few people walking along the shore.

Land felt like another world.

Part of Vicki wanted to stop paddling, wave her hands, and try to get the attention of the land-dwellers. But if she stopped paddling then she and Zeke would slow down, and she feared that would lead to their deaths.

She kept her hands in the water, staring at land. She wanted land. Needed it. If the shark was going to eat her, then it was going to eat her, but she'd never give up until then.

She would get a new start at life and finally make something of herself, be something more than just a pretty party girl.

She'd get to land.

Although he was swimming in light blue water near the surface, Zeke still couldn't see the ocean floor beneath him, only black. He was about to turn forward to face the raft when he caught a glimpse of something swimming at his side.

His heart slammed quickly, *thud thud thud,* and he

swore he saw a large gray caudal fin swerve into the darkness of the sea.

The thing vanished, leaving the ocean empty. Nothing.

Zeke kept his eyes on where he swore he saw the caudal fin until he remembered the beast could swim around and get him from any direction. His limbs shook. He let go of the raft. His calm goal-oriented mind of reaching land vanished.

How short-lived such a mindset of his was.

Fear devoured him, and his back faced the raft as it drifted away.

When his brain started working properly again, the regulator tugged at his mouth. He choked and spat out saltwater.

"Vick. Wait, Vick!"

She kept paddling like she didn't hear him.

After putting the regulator in his mouth again, Zeke grabbed the hose connecting it to the raft and pulled himself back to Vicki. He knew he'd slow her down but he wouldn't—

Right as he looked into the ocean, he saw the top of the great white shark swimming below him, a body length away. It shot right past him, disappearing into the darkness once again.

Zeke knew the shark was fucking with him. It had to be.

Once he reached the raft, he was about to yell at Vicki for leaving him but quickly realized there'd be no point to yelling at her. He'd frozen up while she was determined to live, and he thought maybe, *if just maybe*, one of them could get to shore safely then the deaths of Ray, Anna, Del, Trisha, and Willie wouldn't be for nothing.

He couldn't let that one person be himself, not after all the selfish things he'd done. The chronic-masturbating asshole survives and no one else? That was not the ending his friends deserved, so filled with fear or not, Zeke forced himself to stay in the water, to keep paddling, to—

His eyes lit up. The sandy ocean floor came into his view.

He'd easily see the shark in the light blue water.

But since land was so close, the beast wouldn't still attack. Right?

While his face was turned to the side, he swore he saw a dark speck approaching him. He squinted as he stared. The speck grew larger with every second passed until the shark's face became clear. It glided calmly through the waters.

Leisurely, even.

Before Zeke knew it, the shark was close enough for him to see its lifeless eyes searching for his soul.

His hand stiffened around the knife.

Vicki relaxed a little, knowing Zeke was behind her pushing the raft once again. She could make out waves crashing to shore a short distance ahead.

People were on the beach, having a great day with friends and family.

She wanted that, needed that, and paddled fiercely to reach the next chapter of her pathetic life.

The dorsal fin cut across the surface, just feet in front of her.

Vicki couldn't stop herself from screaming, and even though she was so close to shore, she pulled her hands out of the water and stopped paddling.

People on land were standing, looking at them, pointing at them.

They couldn't help. No one could.

Zeke swam, knowing his only chance for survival was to

keep moving. If the shark wanted him, it would have him, but he'd make the fucker work for it.

Its caudal fin swerving side to side, the shark swam past Zeke. He couldn't tell if it'd even noticed him.

Don't be silly, he told himself. *Of course it noticed me.*

As it glided away, he knew he had to come up with a plan of attack in case—

The shark cut to its side, turning fully around for Zeke again.

Oh fuck, he thought. *Oh fuck, oh fuck, oh fuck.*

He readied the knife in his hand. The shark darted forward, mouth breaking open, white teeth protruding from its pink gums.

Looking into the dark pit of the shark, Zeke knew part of Willie was in there, and Del, Ray, and Anna. And Trisha. The shark had all of them, yet it still wanted the last two survivors of the group.

Zeke readied to be next.

Then, just a few feet in front of him, the monster dashed to the side and swam out of the light blue waters, deep into the dark once again.

One man could only take so much, and Zeke was already beyond his limit. If he wasn't going to make it to land, then he wanted to be dead because he couldn't handle another run in with the shark. Anything in between death and land was torture.

But he kept swimming and inhaled deeply, his muscles tight and warm.

I'm making it home, he thought. *I'm almost there.*

The clear sandy bottom of the ocean was just feet below his kicking legs. He imagined feeling the grains beneath his toes, how soft they'd be.

When Zeke turned around, the last thing he saw was the shark's wide-open mouth.

So close to shore, Vicki prepared to leap from the raft

into the crashing waves she longed for. However, the shark could be right there waiting for her, and that terrifying thought caused her to hesitate.

Then again, the shark could be anywhere. Hell, at the rate that thing was killing them off, she wouldn't have been surprised if the shark was already on land, hiding beneath the sand until they stepped in front of it.

A sudden slam sent Vicki flying into the water.

She didn't panic, only swam. She had to, couldn't look back, would never look back.

Waves carried her until she tumbled onto the wet sand. She crawled out of the water and rushed up to a stumbling stance. Spinning around, mouth quivering, she screamed his name, "Zeke!" She tripped over herself, fell, pushed herself back up. "Zeke!"

Only crashing waves answered her.

"Zeke! Please, Zeke!"

He'd promised they would feel the warmth of a dry towel. He'd promised her that.

"Zeke!"

People were running toward Vicki, but she kept her eyes on the sea.

Out of the crashing waves, the SNUBA raft tumbled to shore. A large chunk of it was missing. Bitten. Vicki rushed forward, pulled it out of the water, and fell to her knees. She pressed her hands to her chest as she rocked back and forth.

And she cried. She felt she deserved to cry after holding it in for too long. There were too many reasons not to cry: her friends were dead, she was safe, and—

A body flung from the waves, a bloody pool surrounding him.

Zeke reached for her, screaming as he crawled up the shore. His pained eyes stared at her. She scrambled to his reaching hand, and her fingers slipped between his.

A husband and wife were close, sprinting for them.

Rolled over onto his back, Zeke rested his wet head on Vicki's thighs and stared up at her. His eyes rocked side to side. "I, *ha*, I think I did it." In his hand was the steak knife, and the final seconds of a wave washed up to them, soaking them in blood.

"We made it," she said, pressing her palm against his cheek.

Although his teeth were stained red, his smile never looked prettier. "We did?"

Vicki pulled Zeke close enough to kiss him. Right before her body gave out, a dry towel wrapped around her back.

the end

EPILOGUE

You might be wondering how I, Elijah Augustus, survived that cruel exploding boat.

Well, you won't like this, but sometimes the easiest answer is the simplest one, the one right in front of us. So I'll tell you how I survived:

I just did.

Poor Alicia, but as wise men say, when one door closes another opens.

Having a drink with my faithful companion Dickens, I said, "Dickens, my boy, we have done it again."

Dickens let out a little puff of air from his small lips. No one would ever know what he said but me.

After finishing my drink at the Tiki Bar and Grill, I said, "Another successful run."

Dickens gave me a nasty stare.

"What, you don't think so?"

His small wrinkled face was blank but noisy.

"Oh, okay, so we didn't get the shark. So Quenty met his fate as well as my delicate flower. Maybe you are right, Dickens, but me and you, we continue on. We fight the good fight. The fight between man and beast."

Dickens said nothing.

The weight of the bar crushed my shoulders like it wanted to drown me in my empty drink. "This war will never end," I said. "Will it, my friend?"

The bar doors swung open. Gasps filled the room.

I turned around after finishing my drink to see a drenched girl in a tankini top hunched over, fighting for air. Her dark hair was soaked around her head and face.

Before collapsing to the floor, she screamed, "Help!"

The few others in the bar rushed to the girl.

I walked over and hovered above the crowd. The girl was fighting to stay awake, and she had a nasty bite wound, a bite wound I was quite familiar with.

I shoved everyone aside, knelt over the girl, and gave her a gentle whisper, "What happened, sweet babe?"

Her weak face pressed against the side of mine. "He-help."

"Tell me what has wronged you."

"Sh…." The girl's lips trembled. "Sh…."

I raised an eyebrow. "Sherlock Holmes?"

The girl's eyelids fought to stay open; they shut for a second, but then she thrust a hand around my neck. "Sha—"

"Sheep-faced salamander?"

The girls screamed one last time, "SHARK!"

I jolted to my feet and nodded at everyone else. "I'll find your shark. I'll kill your shark."

A scrawny man to my right grabbed my wrist. "Who the hell are you?"

"I'm Elijah Augustus." I grabbed the face of the man-full-of-questions. "Shark hunter."

He said nothing.

I leaped over the dying girl, yelling, "Come, Dickens, we have work to do!"

Out on the beach, staring at the ocean, I knew what must be done. Only one goal needed to be accomplished. I wasn't talking about drinking delicious drinks or twolly-popping around the beach. No, my destiny awaited, and I would not fail, for too many innocent people had fallen prey to those beasts in my ocean.

With wind blowing through my beautiful lion's mane of hair, I prepared for the deadliest of voyages. Dickens was ready, so was I.

Ready to slay....

TWO PISSED-OFF SHARKS

(Possibly coming soon)

www.ingramcontent.com/pod-product-compliance
Lightning Source LLC
Chambersburg PA
CBHW021045130626
46552CB00005B/2026